CAUGHT IN THE MIDDLE

JENNIFER HAYDEN

CAUGHT IN THE MIDDLE

ISBN 10: 1987561252
ISBN-13: 978-1987561258

CAUGHT IN THE MIDDLE

Copyright © 2018 Jennifer Anne Hayden

All rights reserved. Except for use in any review, the reproduction or utilization of this work in whole or in part in any form by any electronic, mechanical or other means, now or known hereafter invented, including xerography, photocopying and recording is forbidden without the written consent of the author.

This is a work of fiction. All characters, names, situations and places in the book are purely from the imagination of the author and have no relation to anyone either living or deceased.

1

Casey Gage slammed his locker shut and reached for the duffel bag that lay at his feet. He was freshly showered, having just finished a twenty-four-hour shift at Station 15, in Seattle, where he'd worked for the past twelve years.

Becoming a firefighter had been a no-brainer for Casey. The Gage family was well dug in with the Seattle Fire Department. Casey's older brother, Trent, and younger brother, Brandon, were firefighters, too, also with Station 15. Trent had just been promoted to lieutenant. Their younger sister, Colby, was a paramedic with 15 as well. Their father, Adam Gage, had been a well-respected battalion chief when he'd retired from the SFD three years earlier.

In other words, fighting fires was in Casey's DNA. He'd never thought of doing anything else—wouldn't consider changing his career if he had the chance. He loved his job. He liked the excitement, the danger. He liked the adrenaline rush when he was up on that ladder, pulling someone to safety.

That being said, there were days when he wanted to go home and pull the covers over his head. There were days when being a first responder sucked. There was no unseeing the horrors of society. And there were a lot of horrors out there.

Today had been one of those days.

Slinging his bag over his shoulder, Casey started for the exit. He wanted nothing more than a warm bed and ten hours of uninterrupted sleep.

"You okay?"

He lifted his head, locked his eyes on his brother's.

Trent Gage was similar to Casey in looks. They shared light brown hair and blue eyes. Casey was slightly shorter than Trent's six-feet-two-inches. Trent was three years older than Casey, at thirty-five. He was the oldest of the Gage clan. No wife, no children. Like his siblings, Trent liked to keep free of entanglements, to their mother's chagrin. She wanted grandchildren and none of her kids seemed to be in a hurry to provide her with any.

"I'm good," Casey said, trying to sound nonchalant. The arch to Trent's brow told Casey his brother wasn't falling for his devil may care attitude.

"I know it was a tough one last night. But I have some news on the kids in that fire. Thought you'd want to hear about it."

Casey lifted a brow, interested whether he wanted to be or not. The truth was, he tried to keep himself detached from the situations he walked into on the job. That was rule number one in first responding. There was a task that needed to be done and emotions couldn't play a part in that task for the most part. Lives hung in the balance.

But the night before, that entire theory had gone to hell in a hand basket. Not just for Casey, he knew, but for all of the firefighters that had been there.

The fire they'd responded to had been a two-alarm. The home, barely inside the city limits, had been up in flames before they'd even gotten there. Two kids, a boy and a girl, had been rescued from an upstairs bedroom. Both had been unconscious. Casey and Trent had been the firefighters to pull the kids out of the burning home. Only when they'd gotten them situated on gurneys, had they realized the kids had been shot. An ambulance had whisked them off to Seattle General Hospital before Casey could ask any questions. He'd gotten back to work, still with the images of their tiny smoke tinged faces in his head.

Further search of the house turned up two more victims, adults this time. A male and a female, both shot in the chest. Likely they'd been dead before the fire had even started.

"Kids are still hanging in there," Trent said, shoving his hands into the pockets of his blue uniform pants. While he was technically off shift now, just like Casey was, he hadn't bothered to shower or change yet.

"That's good," Casey said, feeling a bit of hope. "What are their chances?"

Trent shrugged. "Fifty/fifty. They've got names. Tiffany and Jaden Cowell. Eight and six. Brother and sister. The adult vics were their parents, Lyla and Kevin Cowell. Neighbors have been talking pretty openly with the police. Nice family. Respectful and polite. Nobody saw the fire until it was already out of control."

Briarwood, the neighborhood in which the Cowells lived, was an upper-scale development filled with million-dollar homes. Doctors, lawyers and stock brokers littered the Cowell's block.

"If we hadn't gotten in there when we

did..." Trent's voice trailed off.

Casey knew what would have happened if they hadn't gotten into that house when they had. Both of the kids would have suffered the same fate that their parents had.

"Go home. Get some sleep. I'll let you know if I hear any more." Trent gave his brother a nod and strode toward the showers.

Casey left the fire station and headed for the two-bedroom house he owned across town.

Two years earlier, he'd bitten the bullet and put down roots. The home he'd purchased was about five miles from the house he'd grown up in — the house his parents still owned.

The rambler sat on a small plot in the middle of a nicely landscaped block. The neighborhood was no Briarwood but it was well maintained. The neighbors were all friendly but kept to themselves.

The only drawback to the place was that he'd bought it with his former fiancé. And that fiancé had since become an ex. Unfortunately, even though he'd attempted to buy Kaylee out of her half of the place, she'd refused his offer. She'd simply moved her things from the master bedroom into the spare, where she'd been living for the better part of a year.

Kaylee Simmons was a nurse at Seattle General. She and Casey had met through work. Their relationship had been mutually satisfying for the first year. The minute they'd gotten engaged and moved in together, everything had gone awry. Kaylee had strayed. She'd ended up sleeping with a co-worker—a doctor at the hospital. The beginning of the end of their relationship had ensued. And the sad thing was, Casey hadn't been that upset about it. Sure, his male ego had taken a hit, but pretty quickly he'd felt nothing but relief that the engagement was over. He was more annoyed about their living situation than he was about the breakup itself.

Being a nurse, Kaylee's work schedule was mostly opposite Casey's. Once in a while they found themselves home together on a weekend or an evening. During those times, he managed to make himself scarce.

As annoying as that could be, his only alternative was to move out and let her pay him for his interest in the place. And he wasn't about to do that. He'd been the one to find the house to begin with. He loved everything about it. Sooner or later, hopefully she'd meet some schmuck and move on. So far, no such luck. The doctor she'd been involved with had dumped her recently and she was on the hunt again.

Pulling into the driveway, Casey killed the engine on his truck. He grabbed his bag and headed for the house. Five minutes later, he was in his bedroom, face down on the bed. His eyes immediately closed and he found himself drifting into a dreamless sleep.

. . .

Aria Carlisle glanced around the hospital waiting room. There were people scattered about, some drinking coffee, some sleeping in chairs. Others were chatting quietly amongst themselves. They were all strangers to her.

Taking a lonely seat in one corner of the room, Aria blew out a painful breath.

Over the past three hours, her life had changed dramatically.

A knock on the front door. That was all it had taken.

Sighing, she leaned back and took a moment to gather herself together.

As a child, she'd grown up in Bellingham, Washington. Not far from the coast, the town was mid-sized and sat about an hour from the Canadian border. The house she'd lived in with her parents and siblings had been modest. Her father had been a teacher, her mother a homemaker. They'd lived an idealistic life. At least that's the way it had appeared to the outside world.

Behind the scenes, alcoholism and anger had been a constant elephant in the room. Both of

Aria's parents had dipped into the bottle far too much to be considered casual drinkers. Not only that, her father had had a penchant for cheating. *Women and booze*, her mother had always told the kids. Their father loved nothing but women and booze.

The memory left a sour taste in Aria's mouth and she found herself exhaling painfully a second time.

Adele Carlisle had had many problems of her own. She'd been a drunk herself. Not only that, she'd had a tendency to get violent. She'd been moody and sullen and vindictive. There wasn't a time Aria could remember that her mother hadn't let her children know they were the reason she was stuck in the "stinking, rotten life" she was stuck in.

So, Aria had left home at seventeen. She'd moved to Seattle to attend the University of Washington, gotten her teaching certificate not long after graduating.

And left her family, and all of the volatile memories attached to them, behind.

Until tonight.

Thinking back to the visitor she'd been dragged from her bed to greet just after five that morning, she felt her skin grow clammy.

A police officer.

Aria wasn't the type to attract the attention of law enforcement. The sight of a police officer on her front porch had genuinely baffled her. Even after he'd explained the situation with her sister, she was still baffled. She hadn't even realized Lyla was living in the city, that she'd gotten married, that she'd had two children. Of course it had been nearly thirteen years since she'd spoken to her sister.

Guilt ate at her.

Lyla was two years younger than Aria's twenty-nine years.

Or she had been.

Pain sliced through Aria as she reminded herself that her sister was dead.

It didn't seem possible. Aria was almost unable to wrap her head around the idea. The last time she'd seen Lyla, she'd been a precocious fifteen-year-old. She'd just been getting into makeup and fashion. She'd liked rock music and blasting the stereo in her room until Aria had wanted to pummel her.

And now she was dead.

A myriad of emotions washed over Aria. Again, guilt was prominent. She'd left her sister behind when she'd gone off to college. Sure, she'd written a letter or two to Lyla. She'd always promised to come back and visit her. But a year went by, then another, then another.

Before long, over a decade had passed.

And now here she was, sitting in a hospital, Lyla's only known living relative. At least that's what the cop had told her.

Aria knew she wasn't technically Lyla's only living family. While their father had passed away a few years earlier, their mother was still alive, not that Aria had any idea where she was at this point. And Michael Carlisle, their thirty-eight-year-old brother, was also living as far as Aria knew. Again, she had no clue where. Like Aria, the moment he'd been old enough, Michael had taken off for greener pastures. He'd joined the Army. Because of their age difference, Aria hadn't been close to her brother. He'd never written, never come back to visit. And once she'd left Bellingham, even if he had, he wouldn't have known where to find her.

Aria had occasionally thought about her family over the past several years. She'd even considered getting in touch with Lyla a few times…but she'd hadn't followed through. She was happy with her life the way it was—content. As a kindergarten teacher, she had decent hours, decent pay and summers off. She left for work at seven in the morning and was back home by four. The small house she'd been renting for the past six years was quaint and well maintained, in a pleasant neighborhood near Queen Anne, that was safe and friendly. She liked her neighbors, had even made friends with a few of them.

In other words, the past was the past and she'd chosen to leave it there. Fate clearly had other ideas.

Thinking about her sister—about the way Lyla had died—sent chills up Aria's spine. Someone had shot her. Someone had shot her husband and her children, too. And then that someone had set their house on fire, leaving them to burn inside the inferno. Aria knew that by the time the fire department had arrived on the scene, her sister and her husband had already been dead. By the grace of God, the two children had been rescued alive from an upstairs bedroom.

Jaden and Tiffany—that's what the cop had told her. Her sister's kids. Kids she hadn't even known existed. They were eight and six. That idea seemed surreal. They'd been living in the same city as she had, for the better part of three years. Yet, she hadn't even known they were alive.

She couldn't help but wonder why her sister hadn't tried to find her. Lyla had known where Aria went to college. It wouldn't have been hard, in this day and age, to use the internet to do a people search. Yet, her sister hadn't bothered. Not even after their father had died.

Aria reminded herself that she hadn't searched out her sister, either. There hadn't been a funeral—no reason to go home. It was possible that Lyla had felt the same way about their childhood memories. They were better left in the past.

"Ms. Carlisle?"

Aria was startled out of her reverie. She lifted her head until her eyes landed on the tall, good looking man that stood in front of her. His hair was dark, nearly black, which was a stunning contrast to his gray eyes. He looked official, even in the plain clothes he wore. There was a gun holstered at his side and a badge clipped to his belt. He was obviously a cop.

"I'm Detective Nick Holt. Do you mind if I sit?" He gestured to the empty seat next to her.

Even though she wasn't much in the mood for company, she knew she couldn't really refuse him.

She nodded her response and he slid into the chair next to her. His eyes were intense, but she saw a flash of pity in them.

"I'm sorry about your sister."

She felt her breath hitch as the reality of her sister's situation hit her again. She forced the pang of grief that washed over her aside and met the detective's gaze. "Thank you."

"I spoke with someone at the front desk. The kids are both in surgery?"

"They are," she confirmed and waited for him to say more.

"Look, I know this is a bad time, but I need to ask you some questions about your sister — about her husband — "

"I didn't know my sister well, Detective. I didn't even realize she was living here in the city — or that she was married with children. I haven't spoken to her in nearly thirteen years."

He looked surprised. "You were listed as her next of kin on various documents. I've spoken with her attorney."

"I'm just as surprised as you are," was all she could say.

He studied her face for so long that she felt like squirming. "So you can't tell me anything about her personal life? Nothing about her husband at all?"

She didn't hesitate when she shook her head.

He sighed, clearly disappointed. "Okay. Well, here's what I can tell you. Her husband's name was Kevin Cowell. He was an attorney — that's how we found you. His law firm has copies of their wills."

She waited for him to say more.

"They've been married for nine years," he went on. "She's been stay-at-home mom for a good portion of that time. Other than that, I have no real information. This is an active investigation and I can promise you we will get to the bottom of what happened to your sister and her family. That being said, if you have any information at all that you think might help us, I'd like to hear it."

She felt helpless at that moment. "Like I told you, I haven't talked to my sister in years. I really can't help you."

"What about any other relatives? People who may have known your sister better."

Aria hesitated to mention her mother and brother. They were both unlikely to be of any help to the police. On the other hand, she really had no way of knowing whether her sister had been in contact with either of them over the years. "My mother is alive. Last I heard she was still living in Bellingham. I also have an older brother, but I doubt if Lyla has been in contact with him. He joined the Army when we were fairly young and never looked back."

"So you don't know where he is," he figured out.

"I have no clue. When he first left he was stationed at Fort Benning. That was twenty years ago."

He made a few notes in a small notebook. "Okay. I appreciate the information." He dug into his pocket and pulled out a business card, offering it to her. "Do me a favor and call me if you think of anything else that might help us. Day or night."

She took the card and glanced at it hastily before shoving it into her purse. "Someone shot an entire family in their own home. Didn't any of the neighbors hear anything?"

He frowned. "We're still questioning the neighbors, but so far, no."

It seemed impossible that so much violence could have occurred in a house in a decent, close-knit neighborhood, and nobody noticed or heard anything unordinary.

She quickly reminded herself that she really had no idea what the neighborhood her sister had lived in was like. Maybe it wasn't decent or close-knit, regardless of the fact that Lyla's husband had been a lawyer.

"Over the years, I've seen a lot of pretty horrible things that have happened in neighborhoods where nobody saw or heard a thing." His eyes held an air of sympathy. "It is early on in this investigation. People often come forward as time goes by. Memories clear up and things make more sense to them. We'll see."

He wasn't giving her a lot of hope. She watched him rise, shoving his notebook into the breast pocket of his neatly pressed white shirt. "I'll be in touch," he assured her and walked away before she could say anything more.

2

When Casey woke up eight hours later he felt somewhat rejuvenated.

He climbed out of bed and headed straight for the coffee pot. After he had a steaming cup of brew in his hand, he made his way to the shower. Twenty minutes later, he was fully dressed and feeling human again.

He walked into the kitchen and went to work making himself a sandwich. It was just after three. He was a little late for lunch but with his fast-paced lifestyle he knew he'd be hungry again by six.

Just as he sat down at the farm style kitchen table, the back door opened and Kaylee walked in.

Kaylee Simmons was not hard on the eyes. She was tall and toned, curvy in all the right places. Her short blonde hair was cut in the trendy inverted bob that a lot of women seemed to be wearing these days. She was dressed in the scrubs she wore to work so he figured she was probably just getting off shift.

He gave her a cursory greeting and turned back to his sandwich.

She greeted him back before heading to the refrigerator and pulling out a water from her side of the fridge.

When they'd first split up, she'd come up with the idea of dividing the shelves of the refrigerator in half. He'd gone along with her more to keep her happy than anything else.

"I heard you pulled those kids out of that fire," she said, after taking a gulp of water. She leaned against the kitchen counter and eyed him curiously.

He swallowed some sandwich before acknowledging the question. "Trent was there. We both did."

"They're out of surgery. Girl's doing great. The boy's a little more complicated. He had some internal bleeding. It's touchy."

He felt a pang of sadness. He'd been thinking about the kids since he'd gotten out of bed that afternoon.

"Strange thing—what happened to them.

Who would shoot a couple of little kids like that? It just doesn't make sense."

"No, it doesn't," he agreed, finishing up his food. "You know anything else about their situation?" He figured the question was worth asking. She did work in the hospital after all.

"Not a lot." She frowned sadly. "They're all alone. I was on their floor before I left. Not a soul in sight. No family willing to step up, I guess."

He frowned, too. "There's got to be somebody. Between both of the parents they had to have relatives.

She shrugged. "If there are any, they aren't from around here. I didn't see anyone anyway. I was only there for a few minutes though." She gave him a small smile. "You're a hero. Everybody's talking about you."

He scoffed that off, rolling his eyes. "Like I said, Trent was there, too. And we were only doing our jobs."

"You never have been able to take a compliment."

He didn't reply. Lately she'd been tossing compliments his way every time they crossed paths. He wasn't about to encourage her by accepting them graciously.

"I need to get some sleep. Maybe we can talk later?"

"About what?" he asked automatically.

They'd done all the talking they needed to do a year earlier. The idea that maybe she was ready to pay him his interest in the house crossed his mind and he softened his expression a little.

"Just about things. It's been awhile since we've sat down and had a beer together. It would be nice, don't you think?"

No, he thought to himself, *it wouldn't*. "I've got stuff going on this week. I'll get back to you," was all he said, to keep the peace.

She didn't look happy but she didn't argue. She left the kitchen and he found himself sighing in relief. His phone rang and he glanced at the caller ID. Trent was calling. He quickly answered with a curt greeting.

"You up?"

"I've been up for a while. What's going on?"

"I'm almost to your place. I'm heading over to the hospital to check in on those kids. Thought maybe you'd want to come along."

It wasn't uncommon for the guys to follow up after something like what had happened the night before. Casey had been considering visiting the hospital himself. "I'll be out front."

Five minutes later he was belted into his brother's black 4x4.

Trent made a face when he glanced toward the driveway and noted Kaylee's green Prius parked next to Casey's truck. "When are you going to give up and move out?"

Casey didn't really feel like going ten rounds with his brother over Kaylee. This was a recurring thing. "I like my house," he responded simply.

"Dude, there are a million other houses around this city that are much nicer, in better locations, and *vermin free*."

"I like *my* house," he repeated, stretching his long legs out in front of him. "I found it first. I came up with most of the down payment. Why should I be the one to leave?"

"Because she's a bitch and she isn't going anywhere. She's got to be cramping your style by now, bro."

Casey shrugged. "Not really. We work opposite schedules most of the time. We cross paths sporadically."

"You can't even bring a woman home if you want to. That would be awkward."

Casey couldn't really argue that point. The truth was, he hadn't brought a woman home with him for the past year. If he took someone out on a date, they remained out, or went home to her place. It was annoying. But there was really no way around it.

"You're nuts," Trent said, shaking his head.

"Can we drop the subject of Kaylee, please. It's wrecking my mood."

Trent snorted again. Then he sobered. "The police were by the station. Chief called me.

They're going to want to speak to us, too. This thing could get big. It's a murder investigation."

Casey had been wondering about that. "All I know is what I saw. The bedroom. The two kids. I won't be much help."

"Me, either," Trent agreed, pulling into the hospital garage. "I'm guaranteeing you the place was doused in gasoline. I smelled it clear as day."

Casey had smelled the gas, too. "Maybe if the kids pull through, they can identify the person who did it."

"Maybe. Sounds like the girl's doing better than the boy."

"Kaylee mentioned that." Casey climbed from the truck, once they'd pulled into a parking space.

Both men headed into the ER. They were greeted by several people as they passed. Due to their jobs, they knew most of the nurses and doctors on staff at the hospital.

Making his way up to the nurses station, Casey recognized Patti Walter right away. She was a forty-something RN, who'd been working at the hospital for nearly twenty years. She was graying at the temples now, her dark eyes full of curiosity as she lifted her head and met his gaze.

"Didn't you just get off a twenty-four-hour

shift?"

"I did. I went home and slept for eight hours," he said, giving her half a smile.

Trent nodded in agreement.

She frowned as she continued to stare at them. Then, as though she were reading their minds, she sighed. "They're still alive. Out of surgery."

"I heard. Anything new?"

"Not a whole lot. The boy had some internal bleeding. His situation is a bit more complicated than the girl's. They're both in the ICU. There's no way either of you are getting in there."

He knew the nurses weren't supposed to give out any patient information. HIPAA had rules that weren't meant to be broken, even for close-knit first responders. Casey leaned a hip against the desk. "Any family been located?"

Her expression didn't soften. She glanced at her computer screen, punched at a few keys. Then she met his gaze again. "There's an aunt. Mother's sister. She was here earlier. The police are looking into the situation. Of course social services are involved. That's about all I can tell you."

He knew what happened when social services got involved. Even though it was necessary, it was still disheartening.

"Thanks, Patti," Trent said, motioning for

Casey to follow him. They stepped away from the nurses station. "Nothing too surprising. At least the girl's doing better."

"Yeah," Casey agreed.

As they were striding out into the early September sunshine, they ran into Nick Holt, a local police detective they both knew well. Occasionally the firefighters of Station 15 and the cops of Precinct 16 crossed paths both on the job and off. They frequented the same neighborhood bar, Shady's.

Nick Holt was also their sister's on and off boyfriend. He had been for nearly three years. Nick and Colby were complicated, to say the least. They had split up and gotten back together more times than Casey could count. Currently, they were apart. Casey didn't know the details of the breakup. He wasn't sure he wanted to.

"Well, look what the cat dragged in," Nick scoffed, grinning as he glanced from Casey to Trent. "Perfect timing. I was about to look you fellas up. I need to talk to you about that fire last night."

"We aren't going to be able to help you much," Casey warned.

Nick was clearly disappointed. "What can you tell me?"

"Other than the fact that the place was doused in gasoline, not much. Inspector will get more for you," Trent said somberly.

"I've talked to him already. There was definitely gasoline. Kids were both in the same bedroom?" Nick questioned.

"Yes. They were both on the floor in a corner," Casey replied, his skin chilling a little as he recalled the events of the night before. "I grabbed the girl, Trent grabbed the boy. We didn't realize they'd been shot until we got them down to the street."

"You didn't hear any screaming in the house? Any indication that the parents might have been alive at that time?"

Both Casey and Trent shook their heads. "Nobody found them until the house was stabilized for a search. It was too late for them by then."

Nick looked frustrated as he nodded. "Okay. Well if you think of anything else, find me."

"So, what have you got so far?" Casey pushed. He knew Nick wouldn't compromise his investigation but he'd give him whatever information he could.

Nick shrugged. "Not a lot. Looks like the fire was set sometime between midnight and two AM. Neighbor noticed the smoke shortly after two and called it in. Lucky for those kids, the guy was up getting a drink of water. Otherwise..."

Casey blew out a breath. He didn't want to think about the *otherwise*. "Maybe the kids themselves can give you something."

"Believe me, I'm all over that. Right now, neither of them are conscious. Once they are, I'll have to plow through medical personnel to get to them. You know how it goes around here."

"They have been through extreme trauma," Trent pointed out quietly. "Give them a minute to recover."

"Sometimes a minute is a minute too long in cases like these. It's better to speak to witnesses as soon as possible," Nick said unapologetically.

Casey found himself wondering who was going to go to bat for these kids once they were conscious. "Is it true there's an aunt here that's willing to take responsibility for them?"

Nick frowned. "Who told you that?"

When neither Casey nor Trent responded, Nick swore. "This place is an open book. Nobody can keep their mouth shut."

Casey raised a brow in question.

"Yes, there's an aunt. She wasn't close to her sister—hadn't seen her in years, if she can be believed. Her story is that she didn't even know she had a niece and nephew."

Casey thought that over. "Maybe she's telling the truth."

"Maybe," Nick mused. "But there's a lot to this story that isn't making sense. That's really all I can tell you." His phone rang and he glanced at the caller ID. "I need to take this. Let me know if you think of anything else about last night."

Both Casey and Trent nodded and headed for the garage.

. . .

Aria straightened, stretching the sore muscles in her back as she struggled to find a more comfortable position. The wooden chair she sat in was less than plush. Its seat was vinyl and sparsely stuffed, its back ramrod straight and hard as a rock.

For the past several hours, Aria had been rotating between her niece's hospital room and her nephew's hospital room. Neither child was conscious. Both had been heavily sedated following their surgeries.

Right now, she was in Tiffany's room. The doctor had told her that it was more than likely the girl would wake up first. Her injuries were contained and on the mend. The boy's were more complicated. He was likely to be asleep for a while.

Staring at the little girl, Aria did her best to keep her emotions in check. The child looked small. Of course there were tubes and wires surrounding her little body that only emphasized how tiny she was. Both she and her brother had mops of brown curls that reminded Aria so much of the hair her sister had possessed as a child that it was almost scary. Tiffany's face, round and cherubic, also resembled her mother's.

The beeping of the monitors next to the bed and the whir of the machine that was giving the child oxygen were the only sounds in the room. Aria found herself staring at the little girl in awe. She was still having a hard time wrapping her head around the fact that this child was her sister's daughter.

But she was. There was no doubt about that now.

"Ms. Carlisle?"

The voice startled Aria and she turned. There was a heavyset woman standing in the doorway with a clipboard in her hand. She was dressed in business formal — a blue pantsuit and white blouse. She wore a nametag on her lapel that read Joanne Sutcliffe. The words underneath her name were too small for Aria to read. She gave the woman a questioning look.

"I'm Joanne Sutcliffe. I'm with Seattle General's social services department. Would you mind stepping out into the hall for a moment?"

Aria's brow arched. Social services. This couldn't be good. She reluctantly got up and followed the woman out into the hallway.

"Can I get you some coffee?" Ms. Sutcliffe asked, giving Aria a warm smile. "I imagine you've had a very long morning."

"I've already have four cups. That's my maximum." Aria looped her purse over her shoulder and observed the woman critically. She was taller than Aria's five-foot frame by several inches. Built like a linebacker, her hair was brown and pulled back tightly in a professional looking bun. Her eyes were brown and full of curiosity as they perused Aria in return.

"Listen, I realize this a very trying time for you, but I have to ask you some questions. It's hospital policy. You are the only person listed as next of kin for the Cowell children so…" Her voice broke off and she glanced down at her clipboard. When she met Aria's gaze again, she looked serious. "Are you prepared to take responsibility for the children?"

Aria started sweating. "Responsibility?" She repeated the word and felt a shiver course through her.

"Yes, responsibility," Ms. Sutcliffe said, her eyes narrowing. "At this time, both children are going to remain hospitalized. As you know, their injuries are serious. They are stable. But if that changes, you are the person that will need to make decisions regarding their care. Are you prepared to do that?"

Aria hesitated. The children were strangers to her. She was a stranger to them. It didn't seem right that she should be in charge of making major decisions on their behalf.

"If it makes you feel any better, I've spoken with an attorney at Mr. Cowell's law firm. There is a will. In that will, you were listed as a guardian for the children."

The words stunned Aria and she felt a little faint. "That's not possible."

"It is. I have a copy of the paperwork in my office if you would like to see it." Ms. Sutcliffe gave her a sympathetic stare. "I can see you're shocked by all this. I wish there was some way for me to make things easier for you but there's really not. Someone has to make these decisions and your sister and brother-in-law have given you legal right to do so."

Aria exhaled painfully. She was having a hard time grasping that her sister hadn't bothered to look her up—hadn't bothered to even send her a letter, or call her—yet she'd left her the power to make major decisions about her children. It just didn't make sense. "What about her husband's family?" she finally asked solemnly.

"The police are still looking into things of

course, but as of this point, they've found no family for Mr. Cowell. You are the only person listed in their wills."

Aria felt a little faint. This couldn't be. It wasn't possible. "Like I said, I don't know them."

"You're here," Ms. Sutcliffe pointed out quietly. "And you're all they have right now."

Frowning, Aria blew out a breath. "I'm here because a policeman banged on my door at five this morning and told me my sister died in a fire. All of this..." She gestured around her. "It's all come as a total surprise to me."

"Again, I realize that," Ms. Sutcliffe said awkwardly. "But that doesn't change the current situation."

Aria figured that was true enough. This woman wanted an answer — a commitment. She wanted reassurance from Aria. And Aria just wasn't sure she was capable of providing that.

"Obviously your sister had faith that you would be the appropriate person to handle a worst case scenario for her children. She wouldn't have listed you in a legal document if she hadn't. That's got to be worth something, right?"

Again, the woman had a point. Aria found herself slowly accepting the situation. She really had no choice. "Okay," she relented. "If any medical emergencies arise, I'll take responsibility."

Ms. Sutcliffe looked relieved. "I'll need your contact information. Phone numbers, etcetera."

Aria relayed the requested information, then walked back into her niece's hospital room, tension gripping her shoulders. The child was still asleep, her chest rising and falling subtly as she rested. She looked completely defenseless lying there, unaware of the tremulous situation going on around her. She had no idea her parents were dead, that her brother was hanging onto life by a thread. She had no idea that when she woke up, everything she knew was going to change in a horrible way.

The thought broke Aria's heart. She found herself sliding back into the uncomfortable chair helplessly.

She felt nothing but anxiety. The truth was, she had been responsible for nobody but herself for so long that she wasn't sure how to take responsibility for her niece and nephew. Sure, right now it was just their medical care that she was looking after. But when they got better — when they were no longer required to stay in the hospital — what happened then?

3

The next two weeks went by in the blink of an eye for Casey. On his off days he worked construction with a buddy of his—something he did often enough to make a little extra cash. On his on days, he kept busy around the station.

One particular Friday night, things were quiet. The only call they'd gotten so far involved a turkey fryer that had gone amuck and exploded into some surrounding shrubs in someone's backyard. The fire had been put out quickly. Aside from a few irate neighbors, the situation had been easily contained.

Back at the station, dinner had been prepared. Dane Calhoun was the best cook in the place. A five-year-veteran of the department, the thirty-year-old had been a cook in the military. When he'd joined Station 15, he'd been happy to take over kitchen duty.

Calhoun was a good looking guy. Around six feet, with dark hair and light brown eyes. He'd recently gone through a tumultuous divorce. He had a four-year-old daughter named Brooklyn that he spent every other weekend with.

Tonight, he'd whipped up a lasagna that smelled good enough to tempt even the most devoted dieter. Colby had made garlic bread to go with it. Trent and Casey were the contributors of a simple green salad.

"Don't strain yourselves," Calhoun said, smirking as he set a piping hot dish of lasagna down on the table next to their rather bland looking salad.

"You want to be poisoned?" Colby quipped, stepping up to the table and plunking down the garlic bread. "Keep things simple with these two. A bag of salad is perfect."

Casey made a face at her. "I wouldn't be talking, if I was you."

Colby was the youngest of the Gage brood. At twenty-eight, she was tiny—just over five feet tall. Like the other Gages, she had sandy hair and blue eyes. She probably didn't weight a hundred pounds, soaking wet. But she was tough as nails. Nothing got to her. Even the fire the other night that had gotten to the rest of them hadn't fazed her. She was the best paramedic Casey had ever worked with.

"How old is that salad?" Calhoun asked, still smirking. "You know that bagged salad is one of the biggest offenders of food poisoning. Don't you know how to cut up a head of lettuce yourself?"

Casey flipped up his middle finger. "I have better things to do than cut up lettuce, Calhoun."

Trent nodded in agreement.

"Like what? Scratch Kaylee's back?" Dane grinned from ear to ear.

Annoyed, Casey frowned. He really hated the ribbing he got from his friends about his ex and their living arrangement. "Maybe you should date her, Dane. You're single."

Dane appeared to think that over. "She's not hard on the eyes. But I think I'll pass. I have a couple of rules and not dating a fellow firefighter's ex is one of them."

"What's the other one?" Trent wanted to know, as he sat down at the table and helped himself to a pile of lasagna. Casey followed suit.

"Don't date anyone at all," Dane said wryly and headed back toward the kitchen.

It was no secret that Calhoun's wife had done quite a number on him. Not only had she cheated on him with a fellow firefighter—thus the reason for his transfer to 15—but she'd also taken him to the cleaners in the divorce. She'd been brutal about the house, the cars—and most importantly, their child.

"You can't remain celibate for the rest of your life, man!" Trent called after him.

"Oh yes, I think I can!" came from the kitchen.

Casey took a mouthful of lasagna and let the delicious pasta melt in his mouth. He rarely ate a meal this good unless he went home to his mother.

Colby slid into a chair across from her brothers. "I was at Seattle General today. You remember the kids that were in that fire a couple of weeks ago? The ones who got shot?"

Casey swallowed his food and took a sip of water before he considered his sister. "Yeah."

The truth was, he'd been by the hospital twice now and looked in on the kids. The boy was still in the ICU, apparently in a coma. The girl was doing better. According to Kaylee she was on her way out of intensive care.

"The girl's probably going to be discharged soon. I talked to Patti earlier. Looks like she's doing better every day."

"That's great," Trent remarked, over a mouthful of bread.

"Yeah. Things are still a bit up in the air for

the little boy but he's hanging in there. Doc Ryan seems to think he's still asleep because he wants to be."

Casey considered this. He knew Alex Ryan was a good doctor. He'd been a resident at Seattle General for a couple of years now. "So what's that mean? He'll wake up when he wants to, too?"

Colby shrugged, carefully chewing her food. "I guess. I mean considering the trauma that both those kids went through..." Her voice trailed off. "Patti says the girl doesn't speak. Not to anyone, even the aunt."

Casey straightened. "What about Nick? Anything new in the investigation?"

Colby scowled.

Trent snorted.

"You're not speaking," Casey figured out quickly. While he'd known his sister and Nick were on a break, he hadn't realized things had graduated to the not speaking level.

"Hopefully not ever again," Colby snapped.

Casey frowned at her. "I don't understand what the deal is between you two. For three years, you've gone back and forth with each other. The break ups never last. Why bother?"

"He's an ass," she said seriously.

Trent snorted again.

Casey rolled his eyes. "Until when, Friday? Saturday? Give me a break."

"I saw him with another girl, if you must know."

This didn't seem possible. From what Casey knew of Nick Holt, the guy was hopelessly in love with Colby. He had been since the moment he'd set eyes on her.

"I saw them together, big brother. Nick and some floozy. Last week. Now will you drop the subject. If you don't, I'll be forced to bring up the subject of *your* ex again. And we both know how much you like to talk about her."

Touché, Casey thought, grimacing.

"I don't have an ex you can talk about," Trent said, grinning. "You probably misunderstood the situation with Nick. But even if you didn't, you've been broken up for weeks now. He has a right to date other people, don't you think?"

She scowled at him. "A few weeks is no time at all, Trent. Maybe it is in *man* time. But not *my* time." Disgusted, she got up from the table and carried her plate toward the kitchen.

Trent just rolled his eyes. "This is why I stay single. Women have unreasonable expectations."

Casey couldn't argue with him.

The rest of their shift went by quickly. Casey was able to grab a few hours of sleep, so by the time morning hit, he wasn't that tired. Instead of going home, he found himself driving toward the hospital.

He wasn't sure what was drawing him to the two children he'd help rescue from that fire — pity probably. But all the same, he felt the urge to see their situation through.

. . .

Aria sat in her niece's room, listening to the ticking of the clock on the wall and the beeping of various machines that were still hooked up to the little girl, recording her vital signs.

It was Saturday morning. Over the past several days, Aria had found herself commuting between her house, Shady Acres Elementary School and Seattle General Hospital. She taught her class, went home to change, and then hurried over to visit with the children.

Thankfully, things were looking up for her niece. Tiffany was awake and out of the ICU. The moment Aria had gazed into the child's green eyes, her heart had melted. Lord, the girl was literally the spitting image of her mother at that age.

So far, Tiffany hadn't proved to be much of a talker. She'd been informed of her parents' death. She hadn't reacted at all. She'd remained silent and withdrawn. Aria supposed this was nothing to be shocked about. The kid had been through hell over the past several days.

As for Jaden, he was still unconscious. Doctors had assured Aria that his vitals were improving. He was healing. It would take some time.

Knowing the children were getting better only put Aria's mind at ease marginally. She was still on the fence about what to do with them once they were fully recovered.

That being said, with every moment she spent with the kids, she grew a little more attached to them. The hopelessness of their situation grated on her more and more. She truly was all they had in this world. That weight was a heavy load on Aria's shoulders.

To add more complication to the situation, the police—Detective Nick Holt specifically—had been showing up at the hospital daily. The doctors and nurses had left it up to Aria as to whether he was allowed to speak to Tiffany about the night of the fire. So far, Aria had kept him away. It didn't take a genius to realize that Tiffany was fragile. At the same time, Aria knew that every day that passed, a murderer walked free. *Her sister's murderer.* That idea didn't sit well with her at all.

As if on cue, Joanne Sutcliffe walked into the room, that dreaded clipboard in her hand. Whenever she showed up with that, she had something urgent on her mind. Something urgent that was likely going to throw Aria into a tailspin.

"Is this a bad time?" Ms. Sutcliffe asked, glancing at Tiffany pointedly.

Tiffany didn't acknowledge her presence any more than she'd acknowledged Aria's. She just stared across the room at the window, her expression blank.

Reluctantly, Aria stood and followed the woman out into the hallway.

"Let me start by saying the children are improving from what I've heard. That's wonderful."

"They both have a long way to go," Aria responded tightly. She met Ms. Sutcliffe's gaze. She just didn't have the patience to be polite to this woman anymore. She knew the idea was irrational and misplaced, but she couldn't help herself from blaming the overzealous social worker for the private hell she was being dragged through.

"Certainly. But there is a light at the end of the tunnel. I have some good news. Barring no unforeseen changes to her condition, Tiffany may be discharged by the end of the week."

Aria took the words in and digested them. If she were being honest with herself, she'd been contemplating that idea for a couple of days now. Tiffany's physical condition seemed to improve with each day that passed. But her mental state seemed to deteriorate.

"Ms. Carlisle?"

Aria met the woman's probing gaze. "She's still not speaking."

Ms. Sutcliffe's smile faded into an awkward frown. "Physically, she's nearly fully recovered. The mental part of her recovery is going to take some time. Understandably so, considering what she's been through. Unfortunately, we can't keep someone here in the hospital that is physically well enough to leave. I'm sure you understand."

Aria felt her anxiety ramp up to an intolerable level. "Where is she going to go?" She asked the question that had been eating at her for quite some time.

"Well, that depends on you," the social worker replied solemnly. "Legally, you can take her home with you…if you want to."

Anxiety turned into panic. "I can't take her home with me." The words came out before Aria even realized she had said them.

Ms. Sutcliffe arched a brow. "You're the legal guardian, Ms. Carlisle. I thought I made that clear to you days ago."

Aria exhaled painfully. Guilt was eating at her like a rat gnawing on a piece of cheese. "I can't take her home. I don't even know her."

"It's only been two weeks. That will change

with time."

Aria found herself shaking her head. "I can't."

Ms. Sutcliffe let out a sigh. "Listen, I realize you're overwhelmed. I would be, too, if I were in your position. But you have to understand that if you don't step up here, the child will be placed in foster care. And her brother will be right behind her once he recovers. There's no guarantee they'll be placed together. In fact, I can almost promise you they won't. Is that what you want?"

Aria felt sick to her stomach. She couldn't find her voice to answer.

Ms. Sutcliffe tapped her foot impatiently for a few moments before sighing again. "You should speak to the attorney—the one your sister used to draw up her will. He can explain things better for you. If it's money you're worried about—"

"It's not," she said, cutting the woman off. The truth was, Aria hadn't even taken the time to consider the financial side of things. That only made her anxiety worse. She couldn't support herself and two children on a teacher's salary.

"So, it's that you don't *want* the children," Ms. Sutcliffe figured out. Her voice held a definite note of disapproval, not that Aria could fault her for that. To her, Aria was letting her sister down—letting her niece and nephew down. They were defenseless children, with nobody else in the world to help them. And she was turning them away. She couldn't help but feel disgusted with herself. Still, she couldn't imagine taking full responsibility for two kids at this stage in her life. Two kids she didn't know, that didn't know her, that were suffering with unbearable grief. It was just too much for her to fathom.

"I hope you'll think about this," Ms. Sutcliffe said quietly. "You don't need to make any decisions tonight. You have a few days before Tiffany will be released. As for Jaden, once he's physically recovered, if he's still in a coma, he'll likely be moved to a long-term care facility."

"Long-term care facility," Aria repeated. "What does that mean?"

"We can't keep him here if there is no medical reason for him to be here," she explained. "And before you get upset, I don't make the rules, Ms. Carlisle. I'm merely a liaison between the hospital and you."

Aria found herself scowling. "How will this long-term care be paid for?" She almost didn't want to hear the answer.

"You should discuss that with your sister's attorney. It's possible there is a trust for the children. If not..." She shrugged her shoulders. "There are certainly options. We can discuss those options with you when the time comes. More pressing right now is the situation with Tiffany. Please take a few days to think about this. It's a big decision."

As the woman turned and walked away, Aria felt herself coming undone. As if things hadn't been bad enough for her, now she had a whole new slew of problems to consider.

"Are you the aunt?"

Hearing the male voice behind her, she hesitated before she finally turned around. She wasn't sure who was beckoning her this time, but she wasn't in the mood for any more reality checks.

Surprisingly, she didn't find a hospital staff member behind her. Instead, a man stood in her path. He was dressed in blue cargo pants and a t-shirt with some sort of emblem on it. He was tall. She had to crane her neck to look into his face. And when she did, she was momentarily stunned. He had sandy colored hair and a nice pair of blue eyes that were staring down at her curiously. To say he was handsome would have been an understatement.

She didn't reply to his inquiry. Instead, she narrowed her eyes and stared back at him. Whoever he was, if he was calling her "the aunt" he wasn't likely here with good news.

"My name is Casey Gage," he said, as if that explained everything.

She still didn't reply to him.

"I'm one of the firefighters that pulled your niece and nephew out of the fire a couple of weeks ago."

Suddenly the logo on his shirt made sense. It was the emblem of the Seattle Fire Department. She exhaled slowly and did her best to gather herself together.

It was no use, she knew she still looked like a hot mess. Giving up on redeeming her self-respect, she took a moment and counted to ten inside of her head. Then she forced a smile for him and met his gaze again. "I owe you a thank you. You saved their lives."

He folded his arms over his chest as he leaned against the wall. "I was doing my job," he said quietly. He was looking at her closely, as though he were trying to figure her out.

She wasn't sure what exactly to say to him. She'd extended gratitude to him. What more could he possibly want?

"I've been back here a few times since the fire to check in on the kids. I've never seen you here before."

She frowned. "I work, Mr. Gage. I come here when I'm not on the job. That means nights mostly—and weekends. Is there something I can do to help you?"

He straightened. "How are they? The kids, I mean."

He seemed genuinely concerned so she figured she owed him some kind of answer. "Tiffany's out of danger. Jaden's a bit more complicated."

"Complicated, how?"

"He's physically improving every day. But he's not waking up."

He contemplated that. "So the doctors think this is mental."

"They say he'll wake up when he's ready." She considered him again. She pegged him to be around thirty or so. He had a rugged look to him. It was most likely the firefighter thing. She talked herself out of finding him attractive and gave him another forced smile. "I appreciate you stopping by. I'm glad I was able to thank you for what you did for the kids. Now if you'll excuse me." Finally fatigued, she turned and walked down the hallway and into a small waiting room. The area was empty, thankfully. She needed a moment to herself. She sat down in a chair and took in a deep breath and held it.

Apparently Casey Gage didn't sense her desire to be alone. Either that or he just plain didn't care. He followed her without hesitation. He dropped into the chair next to her as though they were friends. "They're pretty close, your niece and nephew. They were huddled together when we found them in that bedroom."

She lifted her head, the image of her niece

and nephew, injured—terrified, huddled together in the middle of an inferno, now etched into her brain permanently. "Is that so surprising? They're just little kids."

"It's not surprising at all. Neither is the fact that she's not talking and he doesn't want to wake up. Maybe if you put them in the same room together, it will make a difference."

She thought about that and decided the idea had merit. "I don't think the hospital will go for that. He's in the ICU and she's not. They're big on rules around here."

"I know Dr. Ryan. Maybe I could talk to him."

She couldn't hide her surprise. "Why would you do that? You don't even know the kids."

"I don't have to know them to see that they've been through hell. I was there that night. I saw what they lived through. Sometimes there are parts of my job that stick with me—there are people that stick with me. Your niece and nephew—your sister—fit into that category."

She wasn't sure what to say to that.

"Listen, I've got to hand it to you," he went on. "You're in a tough situation here. But the kids are damn lucky to have you. Sooner or later they'll realize that. You're doing a good thing."

She started to open her mouth—to explain

that she wasn't doing a good thing at all. It was on the tip of her tongue to inform him that she was in no position to take on the burden of two children. Two children she didn't even know. At the last minute, she changed her mind. For some reason she didn't want him to know how she was really feeling. She had no idea why. He was a stranger to her. It didn't matter what he thought, and it sure as hell wasn't going to change anything for her.

"I'll let you get back to your family." He stood abruptly. He gave her an encouraging smile that melted a bit of the ice surrounding her heart. "Things will get easier. I know it doesn't seem that way right now, but they will." He turned and walked away, leaving her staring after him with a perplexed look on her face.

. . .

It didn't take Casey long to hunt down Alex Ryan. The doctor had been making rounds when he and Casey ended up in the same elevator together.

"Back again, huh?" Alex said, grinning as he leaned back against the wall. He held an iPad in one hand and a cell phone in the other.

Alex Ryan was in his thirties. He and Casey had known each other for nearly twelve years, ever since Casey had started work at Station 15.

Tall and well built, Alex had dark hair and green eyes. He was easy going and well-liked amongst his peers. He was also very popular with the ladies, although he'd managed to keep himself single up to this point.

"I was just looking for you," Casey admitted.

"I'm going up. Talk to me on the ride," Alex suggested as the elevator doors shut. "You here to see those kids again? The ones from the fire?"

The last two times Casey had come to the hospital, he'd run into Alex. "I poked my head in on them. The boy's still not doing so well, huh?"

"He's doing better physically. There's something else going on there. He should have woken up by now. It's a wait and see thing."

"So put the two kids in a room together."

Alex shoved his cell phone into the pocket of his white coat before he glanced at Casey. "I would have if they were both in the ICU."

"So move him. You said yourself he's physically improved. Move him downstairs and in with his sister."

Alex raised a brow as he crossed his arms over his chest. "Not trying to be rude here, but what makes you such an expert on these kids? You don't know them. Not really."

Casey couldn't really argue with that. "I spoke with the aunt. She thinks it's a good idea, too."

Alex was quiet for a moment. The elevator came to a stop and the doors opened. Alex motioned for Casey to follow him.

"You understand she doesn't really know the kids, either. She didn't even know her sister had kids."

Casey figured he didn't know the particulars about the aunt. Hell, he didn't even know her name. She hadn't given it to him, even when he'd volunteered his. He supposed that didn't really matter. "She's been spending time with them, right? She's going to take them home and raise them. That's got to be worth something."

Alex snorted and turned, leaning back against the nurses station as he eyed Casey. "You're a little out of the loop here, Gage. I shouldn't give you any information but since you're inserting yourself into this mess, I'll fill you in. Aria Carlisle—the aunt—has spent some time here with the kids since that fire. I'll give her props for that. She's taken over medical power of attorney, begrudgingly. But she's not taking custody of those kids. She told our social worker that this morning. She doesn't want the kids."

Casey narrowed his eyes. That wasn't the impression he'd gotten from the woman. Of course she hadn't exactly opened up to him.

They were strangers. "Then what's going to happen to them?"

Alex set the iPad he'd been holding down on the counter behind him and gave the nurse behind the desk a quick order. Then he met Casey's gaze again. "If there's nobody else in the family that's willing to come forward, they'll go into the system. You know how this works."

Casey muttered a curse.

Alex didn't seem any happier than Casey felt. "I agree with you. It sucks. Those kids have been through enough. But the bottom line is that the aunt didn't even know she was an aunt until a couple of weeks ago. She's not a parent herself. Now she's got the responsibility of two children—two extremely traumatized children—in her lap. She's panicking. I'm not really surprised. You shouldn't be, either."

"They're still her family. Her sister's kids. How can she just turn her back like that?" Casey couldn't imagine doing the same thing to any of his nieces and nephews, if indeed he'd had any. He loved his siblings to pieces. There was very little he wouldn't do for them.

"She claims she hadn't seen her sister in years. They weren't close, in other words."

He remembered Nick mentioning the same thing the other day. "That has nothing to do with this. She's all those kids have got."

"Apparently there's a grandmother somewhere. Also an uncle." Alex shrugged his shoulders. "But the police haven't found either of them yet. Chances are, they're not going to be any more willing to take the kids than the aunt is. Some families are like that."

Casey couldn't hide his disgust.

"I hear you, man." A nurse walked over and handed Alex another iPad.

"Results from room 313," she said quickly and disappeared behind the counter.

Alex took the device and dug into its database.

Casey let out a sigh. "All that aside, you could still try putting the kids in the same room together. It's like the twin baby thing. Sometimes all it takes to turn the sick one around is the other."

Alex lifted his head and met Casey's gaze. "I'll give it some thought. The kid doesn't really need to be in the ICU anymore anyway." He paused, his brow furrowed. "This one really got to you, didn't it?"

Casey couldn't deny that fact. "You didn't see what they were pulled out of. Some things stay with you."

Alex nodded in agreement. "I hear you. I'll see what I can do."

4

After her run-in with the fireman, Aria headed to the cafeteria and grabbed a cup of coffee. It was nearly noon. She hadn't eaten breakfast — had no desire to eat lunch, either. Her current situation was getting to her. No matter how hard she tried to convince herself she had every right to walk away from the situation — to turn the kids over to the state — she couldn't.

Damn Lyla anyway.

Guilt ate at her as she cursed a dead woman. Clearly her sister hadn't planned on dying. She probably hadn't figured her will would be executed until the children were grown and living on their own.

Anger coursed through Aria anyway.

Sighing, she sipped her coffee. The more she thought about things, the more she knew she needed to check into speaking with her sister's lawyer. He was likely the only person that could answer any of her questions.

Taking out her cell phone, she made a quick call to Joanne Sutcliffe, who was only too happy to relay the lawyer's information to her.

Once she'd hung up with the social worker, she stared down at the number she'd scribbled on the back of a gum wrapper she'd found in her purse. It was Saturday. Lawyers didn't work on Saturdays, did they?

She dialed the number anyway. She was surprised when a man answered after the second ring.

"Daniel Ronson," the curt male voice said.

Aria took a deep breath. "Mr. Ronson, my name is Aria Carlisle. My sister was Lyla Cowell. I understand you were her attorney."

"Ms. Carlisle. Yes, I've been expecting your call."

If that were the case, she wondered why he hadn't called her himself. Obviously he knew she was listed in the will as a guardian. It would have been nice if he'd let her in on that information before she'd been blindsided by a hospital social worker.

"I apologize for all this confusion," he said, as though he could read her mind. "What happened to the Cowells—your sister and her husband—it was awful. Just awful. I'm sorry for your loss."

"I appreciate that," she said tightly. "But as you can imagine, I'm calling regarding the children. I've spoken to the social worker here in the hospital. Joanne Sutcliffe."

"I've spoken with her as well," he replied.

She thought her next words over very carefully. "I'm sure you can understand why I would question what she's told me."

"I'm not sure what information she's shared with you. For medical purposes, I did let her in on the guardianship situation that your sister outlined in her will. Mr. Cowell's will reads the same. They requested that you take responsibility for the children in the event that anything should happen to them."

She'd expected to hear the words, but still they caused her to start sweating again. "That's where I'm confused," she said honestly. "I haven't seen my sister in thirteen years, Mr. Ronson. I didn't even know she had gotten married—had kids. This situation just isn't acceptable."

Mr. Ronson was quiet again. Then he sighed. "I'm not in the habit of handling a case this precarious over the phone, Ms. Carlisle. Perhaps you and I should meet."

"Perhaps we should," she agreed. "Sooner

rather than later. The children are improving. And while this is certainly good news, arrangements need to be made for them by the time they're released from the hospital."

Again, she received silence. "I don't usually work on weekends," he eventually said. "I only forwarded the phones here today because I had an important conference call I had to take."

Annoyed, she scowled. "I can assure you, this won't take long. I need to see that will. And arrangements for those children need to be made. I consider this an emergent situation. I work fulltime during the week so weekends are more convenient for me." She was rarely so forthright with anyone. At this point, she didn't care if he got mad or not. He wasn't the one being forced to turn his life upside down.

"Very well. I suppose I can meet you at my office. It's on 2nd Street." He rattled off an address. "Two o'clock?"

She agreed and disconnected the phone. The meeting with the attorney hadn't really been on her agenda for the day but she knew it had to be done. The sooner she ironed out this mess, the better she was going to feel.

After hanging up with the attorney, she headed back to Tiffany's hospital room. When she got there, she was surprised to see a flurry of activity going on. When she looked for the bed her niece had been lying in for the past several days, she saw that it was gone.

Confused, she turned to a nurse, who gave her a sympathetic smile. "She's just down the hall. Follow me."

Aria did as she was told. Three doors down, she was led into a different room, this one much larger, with a nice big window that looked out over the city scape. There were two beds in this room. In one, Tiffany lay. In the other, was Jaden, still unconscious. At least it appeared that way.

Stunned, she stared from child to child. And then it occurred to her.

The fireman.

This had to be his doing. He'd told her he was going to talk to Dr. Ryan about putting the kids together. Obviously he'd made good on the promise.

"Is he going to be okay?"

Hearing the words, Aria turned, stunned. Tiffany was staring up at her, green eyes wide and curious—and full of worry. She glanced at her brother. "I thought he was dead, too."

Sadness and regret washed over Aria, at the same time as a swarm of relief did. Finally, her niece was talking.

She walked over and set her purse on the table in between the beds. "He's getting better, sweetie," she heard herself saying. "I mentioned that to you. Why did you think he was dead?"

Tiffany shrugged her tiny shoulders. She looked over at her sleeping brother. "Because he was gone. Just like Mommy and Daddy. He was just...*gone*."

Aria felt a lump form in her throat. "Do you remember who I am?"

Tiffany kept her eyes on her brother. "You're Aunt Aria. Mommy's sister."

Aria was relieved to know the girl at least knew who she was. "That's right. How are you feeling?"

Tiffany shrugged.

Aria took a seat in the chair next to the bed. "I'm sorry you thought your brother was..." Her voice broke off. She couldn't get herself to say the word. "I thought you understood he was in a different room. The doctors were watching him more closely so he would get better faster."

"He's still sleeping," the little girl said quietly. "Why isn't he opening his eyes?"

Aria glanced at Jaden and blew out a breath. "Because he's healing, honey. Sometimes getting well takes a lot of energy. I think he's going to open his eyes soon. We just have to be patient."

Tiffany nodded solemnly.

Aria was at a loss for words. She'd thought the one-sided conversations she'd been having with her niece were awkward. But now that Tiffany was talking, things seemed even more strained. "Is there anything you need? I'm going to go out for a bit and I can bring you something back. Maybe a favorite book or a magazine?" If the girl was eight, she likely was reading at least at a second grade level. Aria remembered her sister being an advanced reader at that age. Perhaps Tiffany took after her mother.

Tiffany just shrugged. "Jaden likes *Captain Underpants.*"

Aria had heard of the popular children's books. She made a note to pick out a couple when she got a chance.

"Am I going to live with a stranger?"

The words shocked Aria and she sat there in stunned silence for a moment. What in the hell was she supposed to say to that? "You don't need to worry about that right now," she managed to force out. "You just need to get well."

"I heard you outside the door earlier. You and that woman. She said we're going to foster care. That's strangers, isn't it?"

Aria's heart cracked down the middle. She'd thought she and the social worker had been far enough away from the room when they'd been talking that morning. Apparently not.

"I don't want to be away from Jaden again. Please don't let that happen." Tiffany's eyes were locked on Aria's now. "If we have to go somewhere, please make them keep us together." A lone tear dribbled down the girl's cheek. "You can do that much, right? I mean if you tell them? I've seen that on TV. Brothers and sisters can stay together if you ask."

The child's desperation was Aria's undoing. She had no idea how to respond to her.

A knock sounded on the door before she could come up with an answer and Aria turned her head. She saw Detective Nick Holt standing in the doorway, his eyes intent as he glanced from her to Tiffany and then back again.

"I'll be right back," she told Tiffany, and got up from the chair. She gave Detective Holt a look and herded him into the hallway. This time she made sure they were out of Tiffany's earshot.

"She's talking," he said, when they had reached the end of the hallway. Narrowing his eyes at her, he frowned. "Why didn't you call me?"

"Because she's only been talking for the last hour. I think it's because they moved her brother into the room with her." She gave him a frown of her own. "She's not ready for any kind of interrogation, Detective. Surely you can understand that."

"Two weeks have gone by, Ms. Carlisle. Every day that passes, she's possibly losing more and more of her memories from that night. I need to speak with her. It can't be put off any longer."

Aria wanted to argue with him. But there was another part of her that was just as anxious to talk to Tiffany about that night as he was. "I don't want her scared back into silence."

"Neither do I," he agreed, folding his arms over his chest. "But that doesn't change what I need from her. I have two murders on my hands here. Your sister is one of those victims. Don't you want to know who killed her? — who killed her husband?"

"Of course I do," she said automatically. "But Tiffany's been through a lot. I just want to try and make things as easy on her as I can."

"Is that why you're refusing to be her guardian?"

She met his gaze, annoyed. Disapproval was apparent in his skeptical gaze. "That's none of your business."

He let out a sigh. "I shouldn't have said that. I apologize."

The apology fell on deaf ears. She didn't really care what he thought of her. The problem was, she didn't like the way she was feeling about herself.

"Listen, Ms. Carlisle. I get it. You're a stranger to this situation. But the bottom line is that someone murdered your sister and her husband. That same someone attempted to murder your niece and nephew as well." He gave her a serious stare. "That person is still out there. And they failed. Your niece and nephew are still alive."

She felt her heart begin to pound erratically. "You think whoever tried to kill them may try again?"

"It's possible. They're witnesses to a crime. What exactly they witnessed, I don't know. But if someone shot them to shut them up, they obviously saw something."

Aria's skin pebbled. She rubbed her arms to ward off the chill. "You should have someone protecting them if that's the case. They've been here for two weeks, like sitting ducks."

"They've been perfectly safe here. If I hadn't thought so, I would have taken precautions. But once they leave here…" His voice trailed off.

She had no trouble figuring out what went unsaid. Once the kids left the security of the hospital, they were in a whole different situation.

Anxiety rumbled underneath the surface and Aria did her best to tamp it down. "She hasn't tried to talk to me about that night.

It's possible that she won't talk to you, either."

"Just give me the authorization to try. That's all I'm asking for."

She didn't see any way around that. He was right. It was possible that the children were in danger—or would be, once they left the hospital. "You can talk to her. But only for a few minutes. If she gets upset—"

"I'll do my best not to upset her. But given the situation..."

Given the situation, not upsetting the child was probably going to be impossible.

They both headed back down the hallway and into Tiffany's room.

The little girl lay in the same position she'd been in earlier. Her eyes were glued to her brother's sleeping form. A tray of lunch sat untouched in front of her.

"Lunch is here. It looks pretty good," Aria said, walking over and giving her niece an encouraging smile. "Ham and cheese."

Tiffany didn't even glance at the food. Instead, her eyes landed on Detective Holt.

"Hi, Tiffany," he said, keeping his distance. "My name is Nick."

Tiffany didn't respond. She looked at Aria questioningly.

"Detective Holt is with the police, sweetie. He was hoping to ask you a few questions. Is that okay with you?"

Tiffany shrugged her shoulders.

Detective Holt took the lead. He gave Tiffany a small smile. "I know you've had a tough time. I'm sorry about that. But do you think you could tell me about the night of the fire?"

Tiffany didn't even blink. "My mom and dad died."

Aria felt her heart clench.

Detective Holt apparently wasn't shocked by the words because he nodded at the child. "I know. I'm sorry," he said again. Stepping forward, he slid into the chair next to the bed. "Do you know who hurt your mom and dad?—who hurt you and your brother?"

Tiffany bit her bottom lip, then shook her head solemnly.

"Did you see anyone in the house that night, Tiffany? Anyone other than your own family?"

Again, the child shook her head.

"But someone hurt you and your brother," Holt prodded. "And someone set the house on fire. You didn't see that person?"

"It was dark. I was scared," Tiffany said, her voice cracking. "I was trying to protect Jaden. But he got hurt anyway. The bad man hurt him."

"Just one man?" Holt asked carefully.

Tiffany nodded.

"Can you tell me what the bad man looked

like? Like what color his hair was? How tall he was? Maybe what he was wearing?"

Tiffany shook her head. "He had a hat on. I didn't see his hair. But his eyes were blue. And he was angry." Tiffany's lower lip started to tremble. "When he saw us, he got really, really mad..." Her voice trailed off and she shut her eyes tightly. "I want to go home." She started to cry then. Aria's heart broke for what the little girl had been through—what she was going to have to keep going through.

Holt stood up, his gaze sympathetic. He stepped back and let Aria move forward. When she reached for the little girl's hand, the child snatched it back and buried her head in her pillow. At that moment, Aria felt completely helpless.

Holt gave her a look and indicated that she follow him out into the hallway. Reluctantly, she did so.

"She knows who shot her—who shot her family." He said the words quietly.

"If she knows, why not just tell you?"

"She's scared to death. But the more comfortable she gets with us—with *you*—the more she's likely to open up. We have to keep trying. If I can get a description out of her—something more concrete than a 'bad man with a hat', it will help."

"And if you can't?" she asked, folding her

arms over her chest uncomfortably.

"I'm checking into your sister's background, her husband's. So far, I haven't found anything questionable. They both appear to have been model citizens. But this wasn't a random hit. Having those kids talk will expedite this a lot. I need their help."

She knew he was speaking the truth. Nodding her head, she let out a sigh. "I'll try talking to her more. But I'm not sure how this is going to play out, Detective. I'm not going to lie about that. My sister, whether she meant to or not, has left me in a very difficult situation. I'm at a loss here."

"But you're still considering your options," he figured out.

"I am."

"What about your mother? We did finally make contact with her. She's in Bellingham, like you said. Would she be an option for the kids?"

Aria was a little surprised to hear the police had located Adele. She forced her expression to remain impassive. "No. My mother isn't an option."

He raised a brow.

"There's a reason I haven't spoken to her in years. Leave things at that."

"What about your brother? We haven't managed to find him yet but—"

Thinking about Michael wasn't any more encouraging. "I have no idea where he is. I told you that before. It's unlikely he'd take the kids even if you did find him."

"So you're their only hope," he said point blank.

She nearly flinched. "I'm speaking with my sister's attorney this afternoon. That's all I can promise you right now."

He stared at her for a long moment, then sighed. "Okay. I should warn you, I'll be back tomorrow. And the next day, and the day after that. Until I get what I need, I'll keep coming back. I have no choice." With that, he turned and walked away.

He was a cop with a job to do. She couldn't really fault him for that. He was right; Tiffany likely knew who had killed her parents—who had shot her and her brother and set their house on fire. Until she told the truth about that night, she and her brother were still in danger.

That thought sent a chill down Aria's spine. For the past two weeks, she hadn't given herself much chance to consider that side of things. If she agreed to take guardianship of the kids, she would be putting herself in danger, too.

Another strike against the idea.

Shoving the thought aside, she headed back to her niece's room. She spent a few more minutes there, doing her best to get Tiffany talking. Unfortunately she failed. The kid was off in her own little world again, not that Aria could blame her. An eight-year-old wasn't equipped to handle memories like the ones Tiffany had stuck inside her subconscious.

Admitting defeat, Aria headed out for her appointment with Daniel Ronson. She really didn't know how much help the man was going to be, but she knew she owed it to her sister to hear him out.

. . .

After his visit to the hospital, Casey went home and headed out on a run. He tried to exercise most days of the week. Rather than spending his time at the gym, he chose to run outdoors. His favorite route was down on the pier. Five miles roundtrip. The view was breathtaking and that made the trek go by that much faster.

By the time he got back to his house, it was late afternoon. When he pulled into his driveway, he noticed a car parked at the curb. As he climbed out of his rig, he saw Nick Holt sauntering up the walk.

Casey let the door to his truck slam and considered his friend. "If you're looking for Colby, she's not here." He folded his arms over his chest and grinned halfway. "And that's probably lucky for you because you're on her shit list."

Nick muttered a curse and came to a stop in front of Casey. "I didn't *earn* a spot there."

"She says you did. Who's the chick?"

Nick raised a brow. "Dare I ask you to explain that question?"

"Colby says she saw you with some other girl last week."

Nick frowned. "The only girl I've been around lately is Melanie, a new police detective on the force. I was showing her the ropes, took her to lunch one day. Your sister's nuts."

Casey could see the truth in Nick's eyes. He continued to grin. "I don't understand why you haven't put a ring on it, dude. You know that's what this is all about."

Nick rubbed a hand over the back of his neck as he let out a sigh. "If we weren't at odds so often, I might have. She's tough, man. I love her, but she's tough."

Colby always had been tough. She'd been a force to be reckoned with even as a kid. She liked getting her own way. Being the baby of the family, she'd usually gotten it.

"She's got her own way of thinking," was all Casey said.

"That's an understatement." Nick shoved his hands into his pockets. "Listen, I'm not here about Colby. I just left the hospital. The girl is talking."

"The one from the fire?" Casey asked,

surprised. "I was there earlier this morning myself. She was still catatonic."

"Well when I showed up there this afternoon I walked in on her talking to her aunt. Took me a while, but I finally got the aunt's approval to question the kid."

This was interesting. Apparently things had drastically changed for Tiffany Cowell in the past few hours. He wondered what had turned her around.

"She didn't give me much information," Nick went on. "Just that a bad man wearing a hat killed her mom—and he was big and had blue eyes."

"Huh," Casey said, thinking that over. "I talked to Alex today. I thought maybe putting the kids in a room together would help."

"So that was your idea. I wondered who came up with that. I've got to give you credit, it was a good one. I think the girl thought her brother was dead until she actually saw him."

"So they're together now?"

Nick nodded.

Casey was glad that Alex had given the idea a try. "Give her some time. She's only eight."

"I realize that. But the longer she doesn't talk, the more dangerous this situation becomes."

"Because you think whoever shot the Cowells—whoever set that fire—may try to hurt the kids again?" The idea was disturbing.

"It's possible. Word's out now that the children are recovering. That's why I'm here. Are you sure there's nothing about that night you can tell me that might help? I mean anything."

Casey thought back to the night of the fire. He'd been doing that a lot lately. Still, nothing stuck out in his mind that he thought would help the police with their investigation. "Sorry, man. I'd tell you if I had anything for you. To be honest, everything happened pretty fast. We were in and out of there before I could really give looking around much thought."

"I figured. It was worth one more shot." Nick turned to leave.

"What's the aunt's real story?" He wasn't sure why he was asking. He'd heard bits and pieces about Aria Carlisle over the past few days—most of which wasn't good. Meeting her that morning hadn't really cleared any of the mystery surrounding her up for him.

Nick folded his arms over his chest and eyed Casey curiously. "What kind of information are you fishing for?"

Casey frowned. "General information. What's she do for a living? Where does she live? That kind of thing."

Nick grinned. "Is this the professional side of you asking, or the personal side?"

"Don't be a dick."

Nick chuckled. "She's a kindergarten teacher. Twenty-nine. She lives in a rental a few miles from Shady Acres Elementary School where she teaches. No husband, no significant other that she's mentioned. Clean record."

Casey took in the information.

"You interested?"

"Not in the way you're thinking."

"She's cute," Nick said thoughtfully. "Probably not your type though. She has a brain."

Casey flipped his middle finger up. "I'm not interested in dating her, asshole. I'm just curious because of the kids. Alex told me she's not willing to take them in."

Nick sobered. "I think she's on the fence there. I can't blame her. The sister didn't even warn her about the fact that she was designated as a guardian. That's a lot to have thrown at you out of nowhere."

"I suppose. She's still the only family they have left."

"You're preaching to the choir," was all Nick said.

Casey watched him leave. He considered the situation again. He supposed Nick was right; it was a lot to handle out of the blue. But still…

Tossing his keys in his hand, he headed for the house to change.

5

Aria pulled her car to a stop in a parking spot near the front doors of the building that housed the law offices of Ronson, Armbrust and Booth just before two o'clock.

Daniel Ronson had told her the front doors would be unlocked. There were several other businesses in the building that were open on Saturdays. Once she took the elevator to the fourth floor, their suite was to the left. He was going to leave the door unlocked for her. His office was the last door to the left.

Following all his instructions, she found her destination easily enough.

The suite of offices was new and modern. The décor leaned toward contemporary. There was a large front reception area that was empty, due to the weekend. On the wall behind it, in large, gold letters, was the name of the firm. Aria imagined the place was probably bustling with activity during the week. Today, it was like a ghost town.

"Can I help you?"

Startled, she jumped and whirled around. A man stood behind her, dressed casually in jeans and polo shirt. He was tall, probably around six feet or above. He looked to be in his late thirties with blond hair. His gray eyes were curious as they observed her carefully. His voice did not match the voice she'd spoken with earlier over the telephone. This man couldn't possibly be Daniel Ronson.

"My name is Aria Carlisle. I'm here to see Mr. Ronson," she explained quickly.

"Really. Daniel doesn't work on weekends." He leaned back against the reception area. "Is there something I can help you with? I'm Brad Armbrust."

She put two and two together and figured this man was likely another partner in the firm. He seemed pretty young to be in such a prestigious position but looks could be deceiving.

"Mr. Ronson's expecting me," she said eventually, a little annoyed that she was being waylaid. "I have an appointment with him at two."

"Is that right?" He was thoughtful again as he checked his watch. Then he shrugged. "He's probably running late then. I just got here myself and nobody else is around. You can sit down here if you want. I'm sure he won't be long." He indicated to a small waiting area filled with a row of comfortable looking chairs.

Quickly realizing she had no choice, she was about to sit down when the door behind her opened and another man walked in. This guy was much older than Brad Armbrust, probably in his sixties. He was tall and gray, with a well-trimmed beard covering his jaw. He was dressed in an expensive looking suit, a definite contrast to his partner. He reminded Aria a little bit of Santa Claus. When he saw her, he gave her an apologetic smile.

"Ms. Carlisle?"

She nodded, thankful for his presence.

"Brad," he said, acknowledging his partner. "Working on Saturday, huh?"

"I could say the same thing to you, Daniel. Anything I can help out with?"

Aria watched as Daniel Ronson considered his partner for a moment, then shook his head. "No. This is routine. If I leave last, I'll lock up."
He motioned for Aria to follow him down a long hallway, which she did. His office was tastefully decorated, just as the lobby had been.

Various awards and achievements were on display around the room. Aria took a moment to glance at them.

"I apologize for my tardiness. I got hung up at home and traffic was bad today—but then it always is." The man set a briefcase down on his desk and considered Aria seriously. "Now then. I should formally introduce myself. Daniel Ronson." He held out his hand to her and she reached forward and gave it a cursory shake.

"Have a seat, please," he said, indicating the chair across from him. Once she was seated, he sat down, too.

Slipping a pair of wire-rimmed glasses over his nose, he dug through a pile of paperwork that rested in the middle of his desk.

"Let's start by having you take a look at the will." He lifted his head, met her gaze. "I assure you, though, that I've been completely straight with you. There will be no surprises here."

"This whole thing is a surprise," she muttered, taking a thick packet of stapled papers from him.

"I'll be honest with you, Ms. Carlisle. I didn't know your sister well. I worked with her husband—fairly closely, in fact. Kevin Cowell was a good man. Hard working. He was next in line for partner." He looked regretful. "He was one of those people that always went the extra mile. That's what I liked about him."

"I never met him," she admitted.

"I gathered as much." He set his glasses down on the desk and eyed her with interest. "Your sister was a supportive wife, from what I saw. She accompanied him to the necessary parties and events. She was involved in community affairs. She was an asset to his career, if that doesn't sound too crass. She fit in with the other wives around here just fine."

She thought that over. The last time she'd seen Lyla, she'd been a teenager. It was hard for her to imagine her sister as anything other than that.

"She loved her kids. Kevin talked about that all the time — about how important they were to her. About how good of a mother she was."

Aria didn't doubt that. When they'd been young, she and her sister had always promised to be the exact opposite of their own mother.

"So what can I do to help you out here?"

Aria skimmed the pages of the will. She knew she didn't have the time to read it word for word.

Ronson gave her a few minutes, then cleared his throat. "There's a lot to the will. The part you need to be concerned with currently is the guardianship." He reached forward and took the document from her, turning several pages before handing it back to her and pointing his finger toward the bottom of the page. "There."

She read the paragraphs he pointed out to her. When she was through, she read them a second time. He was right; there were no surprises. Lyla had listed her as guardian for the children if anything was to happen to her and her husband.

"I understood from our conversation over the phone, you're reluctant to take responsibility for the youngsters."

She was hesitant to say what she'd been telling everyone else who had questioned her about the kids. In the end, she really had no other answer. "I don't know anything about kids, Mr. Ronson. Not only that, I'm basically a stranger to them."

He leaned back in his chair. "This has come as a total shock to you, hasn't it?"

She nodded, setting the will down on his desk. "My niece spoke today. For the first time since the fire."

His expression brightened. "That's good news. What about the boy?"

"He's still in a coma. The doctors are hopeful. The kids are together now. That may make a difference."

"I only met the children once." He steepled his fingers in front of him. "I regret to say that this firm isn't the most family friendly place on earth. We're a law firm. It doesn't suit clients well to deal with hooting and howling children when they come in here for a meeting."

"I suppose not," she agreed. She rubbed at her throbbing temples. "I'm not sure what to do here. I want to do the right thing. I really do. But this is complicated."

"It is," he agreed. "Your sister should have notified you when she put you in the will. That being said, the papers were only drawn up a few months ago. Maybe she planned to and just didn't get the chance."

Aria supposed that was possible. That really didn't change anything for her though. "There are a lot of bills here. Hospital related. If Jaden doesn't wake up soon, he'll be sent to a long-term care facility. I'm not sure how to handle all that."

"It will be taken care of," Ronson said without hesitation.

Surprised, she met his gaze. "How?"

He didn't even blink. "We take care of our own. The children have decent insurance. What isn't covered, we'll take responsibility for." He dug through his paperwork. "You should also know there is a sizeable bank account. I've been handling the probate, so I can give you all that information. If you should agree to take guardianship of the children, all that will be yours." He met her gaze. "The house was paid for, which given its current condition is a good thing. There will be an insurance settlement. They have multiple cars that are paid off as well. There's also a vacation property near the ocean."

Surprised, Aria stared at him in awe. "A vacation home?"

"I just signed the paychecks. I didn't spend their money," was all he said.

She took a minute to digest all of this. Her sister had been married to a very rich man. A rich man who appeared to be well-respected, well-liked. She felt her lips quirk with respect. Good for Lyla. She'd done alright for herself apparently.

"The only question here, Ms. Carlisle, is if you're willing to become a guardian for the children."

She wanted to say yes. She knew it was the right thing to do. But she still felt apprehensive.

He cleared his throat. "It's pretty difficult to get a child back, once they end up in the system. It's good for you to know that now."

"I realize that."

"You've got a few days. The social worker assured me that neither child will be released before Tuesday at the earliest."

Three days. She had to make a decision that was going to dramatically affect three lives, in three days. Panic threatened again.

"For what it's worth, I understand your apprehension. You're looking at a big responsibility."

That was an understatement.

Gathering her purse together, she stood. "I appreciate your time, Mr. Ronson. And I apologize for dragging you into the office on a Saturday."

He rose, too. "I'm happy to help in any way that I can. You think things over and let me know what you decide."

Aria nodded and turned to leave. She didn't get two steps outside Mr. Ronson's office when Brad Armbrust appeared out of nowhere. He leaned against a doorway across the hall, smiling, though the smile didn't really seem to reach his eyes.

"Have a good day, Ms. Carlisle." The words came out quietly. For some reason, Aria felt a chill in the air. She barely nodded at him as she walked by and headed for the exit as quickly as she could.

6

After Casey's conversation with Nick in the driveway, Kaylee had pulled up. She had the rest of the day off—lucky him. Avoiding any real conversation with her, he'd showered, changed and headed for the fire station—his home away from home. He had friends on second shift and also his brother.

When he strolled into the kitchen, there were a few guys he recognized lounging around. Apparently things had been quiet that day. After greeting a few people, he searched out his brother, who as it turned out, was napping in the sleeping quarters.

Brandon Gage was thirty years old. He had the same sandy hair and blue eyes as his siblings. That was where the similarities ended. Brandon was the mellowest member of the Gage family. Getting his temper going was nearly impossible. He took pretty much everything in life with a grain of salt. Sometimes Casey wished he looked at the world that way himself. Unfortunately, he didn't.

Giving his brother a kick in the foot, he sat down on the bed next to his and waited.

Brandon opened one eye. When he saw Casey, he frowned. "Is it already time to go home?"

Casey chuckled. "You wish. I stopped by to say hi."

Brandon yawned and reached up to rub his hands over his stubbly jaw. "Kaylee's home, huh?"

His family knew him too well. "She is. She's got the day off."

"That's annoying."

"I thought so." Casey leaned back on the bed he was sitting on and folded his arms behind his head.

"This should tell you it's time for you to find another place, dude. You're running away from your own house."

Casey frowned. He didn't really want to hear this from Brandon. Trent's lecture was still fresh in his head. "I'm not moving. She can move."

"She's still in love with you. She's not going to move, bro."

Casey didn't want to hear those words, either. "She's not still in love with me. She's lonely because Dr. Dipshit dumped her."

Brandon snorted. "Good for him. But I hate to tell you this, she *is* still in love with you."

"Don't say that to me again. It pisses me off."

"You're in denial."

"And happy as hell to be there."

Brandon chuckled.

"Nick and Colby are on the outs again. It's not good."

Brandon rolled his eyes. "Gee, that's a shocker."

"I'm serious. I think Nick's getting tired of Colby's up and down attitude. She's accused him of being with another woman this time."

Brandon winced. "Seriously?"

Casey nodded. "The chick is a new co-worker. He was just showing her the ropes. Colby jumped to conclusions. That's Nick's version of the story."

"He's not one for lying."

"No," Casey agreed. He thought about his conversation with Nick. Inevitably, his thoughts strayed to Aria Carlisle and he found himself frowning.

"What?" Brandon asked.

"Nothing. I was just thinking about the kids from that fire a couple of weeks ago. Nick's on the case but so far he's got nothing. He's afraid the kids are going to be in danger now that they're improving—the girl anyway."

Brandon let out a sigh. "It's a shitty situation. Be good if one of those kids could shed some light on things."

"It would," Casey agreed. He started to say something else when one of the guys peeked around the corner.

"You've got a guest, Gage."

Brandon sat up, surprised. "No kidding. Who?"

"Not you." A finger was pointed in Casey's direction. "You. It's a hot chick. You better run before the other guys jump on it."

Casey found himself frowning. He knew most of the guys—even the second shifters—knew Kaylee. So if it wasn't her looking for him then who was it?

"You hiding a secret girlfriend from the family?" Brandon asked, sitting up and raising a brow.

Casey shook his head as he rose. "Not hardly. Mind your own business and go back to sleep."

"I don't think so."

To Casey's annoyance, his brother followed

him out into the garage.

Casey glanced around for a few moments before his gaze landed on a woman standing awkwardly in the doorway. She looked nervous and out of place. Dark hair, green eyes.

Aria Carlisle.

. . .

Aria bit her bottom lip as she contemplated turning around and taking off before Casey Gage appeared. Stopping into the fire station had been a spur of the moment decision. She'd intended to drop off a little token of her appreciation on behalf of her niece and nephew. The man had saved their lives. And that morning, she'd been out of sorts. Hell, she'd been borderline rude.

But now that she was standing here, a box of bakery cookies in her hand, she felt silly.

Bakery cookies? The guy had saved two lives. The gesture suddenly seemed very lame.

Several men sauntered into the garage, all observing her curiously. Her nerves unraveled a little bit more.

"Don't you jerks have something to do?"

She glanced toward the doorway that led inside to the main part of the station, and there he was.

That morning when they'd crossed paths, she'd noticed how good looking Casey Gage was. He'd been dressed in his uniform at the time. Now he was not. He was wearing a pair of faded jeans and a t-shirt, a pair of sneakers on his feet. His hair was windblown and his jaw was covered with a thick layer of bristle. He was still good looking. Maybe even more so in this casual getup.

Her heart skipped a beat and she felt like slapping herself. She was here for a reason. She would give him a simple thank you and be on her way. Before she could even open her mouth, he was standing in front of her, his arms crossed over his chest. He eyed her curiously.

"How can I help you, Ms. Carlisle?"

The sound of his voice startled her and she found herself exhaling uneasily. He knew her name. She hadn't given it to him that morning. She supposed Dr. Ryan had probably filled him in. She forced herself to look up into his face. Big mistake. Suddenly she couldn't breathe.

"Are you okay?" His lips quirked at the corners and she knew he knew what kind of affect he was having on her. An egomaniac. Great.

She gathered herself together quickly, forcing a smile for his benefit. "You spoke to Dr. Ryan this morning, didn't you?"

"I told you I would. I heard he moved the

kids into the same room."

"He did. Thank you." She offered him the box of cookies.

He stared at it for a moment before accepting it. "What's this?"

"Not much, actually. Now that I'm looking at them, I'm wondering why I grabbed them at all. You might feel insulted."

He surprised her by cracking a smile. "Well since you're making them sound so appealing..."

He had a point. Again, she wanted to slap herself. Why was she acting so irrational? She took a deep breath and tried to redeem herself. "I didn't mean they're not good. I got them at the bakery across town. The one with the giant pretzel out front. I stopped in to grab a treat for the kids—well for Tiffany anyway—" She realized she was babbling and cut herself off. "Never mind. The thought behind the gift was to thank you. And to apologize for my behavior this morning. I was rude and out of sorts."

He continued to grin. "You weren't rude. And you didn't have to do this."

"Yes, I did. You saved Tiffany and Jaden. Twice."

He shrugged his shoulders. "I told you before, I was doing my job. As far as talking to Alex goes, he's a buddy of mine. It was no big deal." Clearly curious, he opened the box and peered inside. His smile grew wider. "Chocolate chip. My favorite."

She arched a brow. "Really? You're not allergic to chocolate or anything, right?"

He chuckled. "No. I'm not allergic to anything that tastes great and is terrible for me."

She found a smile threatening. "Neither am I."

He leaned against the door frame of the garage. "I know I saw the kids this morning, but a few hours have gone by. How are they doing?"

She thought about her conversation with Tiffany earlier. "Tiffany is talking."

"Yeah, Nick mentioned that."

She frowned. "Nick. You're friends with Detective Holt, too?"

"Seattle is a big city but first responders run across each other quite a bit on the job. We have each other's backs. Plus, Nick dates my sister."

She wrapped her head around this information. "Really."

He nodded, straightening. "He giving you a hard time?"

She thought that over. Detective Holt hadn't really given her a hard time. He was doing his job. She understood that, even if she was frustrated with the situation. "He's been reasonable but tenacious. I know the kids are a big part of his case. I've been a bit of a roadblock for him."

"Nick's like a dog going after a bone when he's working a case. That's what makes him so good at what he does. That being said, the kids have to come first. They've been through a lot."

She was surprised to hear the words. "He thinks Tiffany knows who killed her parents — who shot her and her brother and set the house on fire."

"He's probably right. She was in the house when everything happened. Chances are, she saw something. Or Jaden did."

She bit her bottom lip again. Every time she thought about the ordeal her niece and nephew had been through, she felt sick to her stomach.

"Listen, Rome wasn't built in a day. Tiffany's been through a lot. It may take her awhile to come to grips with the situation enough to talk about it. Nick's smart enough to realize that. But I have to warn you, he will keep coming back. He's like a boomerang."

"So I gathered." She glanced at her watch and realized she'd been standing here holding him up from his work for the past fifteen minutes. "I'm sorry. I didn't mean to keep you from your job. I should get back to the hospital."

He straightened. "I'm off the clock. I work twenty-four on, forty-eight off. I was on yesterday. I stopped by here today to see my brother."

She remembered him mentioning that his brother had helped rescue the kids from the fire, too. "I forgot about your brother. You'll share those with him, right?"

He shook his head, a mischievous smile on his face. "He's more of a health nut."

She couldn't tell if he was kidding or not. "Maybe you should go get him so I can thank him in person." It was the right thing to do, she decided.

"He's not here."

"But you just said—"

"I have two brothers, both firemen. And my sister, Colby, is a paramedic. We all work out of Station 15. Brand's on shift right now. Trent's the one you're looking for."

"Oh." She knew she'd never keep all the names he was dropping straight so she didn't even try. "Well I hope you'll thank him for me and tell him I stopped by."

He didn't answer immediately. He was looking at her in a peculiar way. She wasn't sure if something she'd said had confused him, or if he was actually checking her out. She wasn't good at picking up signals from men. A little uncomfortable, she backed up. "I guess I'll see you."

"Yeah," he agreed, still watching her.

She turned and headed for her car, her nerves on edge. Why couldn't she be one of those women that knew all the right things to do and say with men? Instead, she got all tongue-tied.

Chastising herself, she walked across the street. She'd parked about half a block down, due to the no parking zones around the station. Just as she was about to reach her car, she noticed something odd. Her back tire was flat. She walked a little closer and realized it wasn't just her back tire. It was her front tire, too. On both sides. All four of her tires had been slashed.

7

Casey listened in as Aria spoke with Nick about the incident with her car.

An hour earlier, when she'd come back into the station looking pale and confused, he'd reached her first. He'd been on his way out. She'd shown him her car—the four slashed tires—and he'd called Nick immediately.

Now, Nick was listening carefully, a frown on his face. He hadn't said much, but Casey could tell he was thinking things over.

"So you didn't see anyone around?"

She shook her head.

"Have you had any problems lately with vandalism? At your house, with your car?—anything?"

Again, she shook her head.

"Okay. Well it's possible that this was just some kids looking for trouble. This isn't a bad neighborhood. With the fire station open right across the street, it's usually safe enough, but crime happens everywhere."

"It's possible it wasn't some kids," Casey pointed out.

"It is," Nick agreed. "But the alternative is that someone is singling you out." He gave Aria an intent stare. "Any idea who would do that to you?"

She seemed startled. "I'm a kindergarten teacher. I don't usually go around making people angry."

"What about on your way here? Any incidents of road rage? No disgruntled confrontations with anyone?"

She thought that over, then sighed, worry evident on her face. "I've been three places for the most part over the past two weeks, Detective. Shady Acres Elementary School, my house and the hospital. I haven't had time to tick anyone off."

"What about today specifically? Where were you before you stopped in here?"

She took a moment. Then she met Nick's gaze. "I met with my sister's attorney. I don't know how I forgot about that. My head's all over the place these days. I've got a lot on my mind."

Nick looked interested. "How was the meeting? Was anything off about it? Anything concerning?"

"The whole thing was off and concerning," she snapped, clearly losing her patience. "My sister died and left me her kids. I don't even know them." She leaned over and rubbed at her temples."

For the first time, Casey got a look at the turmoil that was gnawing at her. She wasn't as uncaring as Alex had made her sound that morning. He felt a sliver of pity for her. She was definitely in a tough spot.

"Ronson, right? I spoke with him awhile back," Nick prodded.

"Yes," she confirmed.

"Well unless you had some sort of disagreement with him — or he threatened you in some way — I wouldn't think he would follow you here and slash your tires. Do you?"

She shook her head.

"Okay," Nick said, folding his notebook closed and shoving it back into his pocket. "All I can do is file a report. It was probably a random thing, like I said — kids looking for trouble."

"And if it wasn't?" she asked, taking the words right out of Casey's mouth.

Nick looked contrite. "Be cautious — aware

of your surroundings. Park in well-lit places, where there are plenty of people—security." He shrugged his shoulders. "Call me if you have any other problems."

Looking a bit defeated, she nodded.

"I've got to run. I've got to get back to the station." Nick left a moment later.

Casey blew out a breath and considered her. "He's right, it was probably random."

"Maybe," was all she said. She stood abruptly, clutching her purse to her.

"What are you going to do now?" he asked curiously. Her vehicle was useless at the moment. It was getting dark out. He wasn't about to let her walk around by herself outside, especially after what had happened to her car.

"Call for a tow truck. I'll need to get all four tires replaced. I have Triple A. I'll figure things out."

"Call them and ask for the tow. I'll drive you wherever you need to go," he decided. "I'm on my way out anyway."

"That's really not necessary," she said quickly, already scrolling through her phone. "I can call a cab."

"It's late and it's dark. Like I said, I'm leaving anyway." He shrugged his jacket on and grabbed his keys.

"I was hoping to go back to the hospital. That's out of the way. I'm fine taking a cab."

He frowned at her silently until she looked up and met his gaze. "Are you always this difficult?"

She seemed a little taken aback. Then she let out a sigh. "No. I'm sorry. Thank you. A ride would be great."

He waited while she called for a tow truck. As it turned out, Triple A was a bit behind. It would be more than an hour before they could tow the car.

"You hungry?" he asked, when she hung up the phone, again looking defeated.

Caught off guard, she didn't answer him.

"It's almost dinner time. We're stuck here waiting for an hour anyway. We may as well grab something to eat."

"I've caused you enough trouble today. You go. I can wait here. I'll be perfectly safe inside my car."

"You haven't caused me any trouble. I'm hungry. I don't like to eat alone. You're doing me a favor." He wasn't sure why he was pushing the issue—except that he realized he found her interesting. She was attractive, of course. But there was something else about her that had him wanting to know more.

Eventually, she shrugged her shoulders. "I guess if you put it that way."

They walked out to the staff parking lot where his truck sat. Once they were inside and buckled in, he drove toward the pier. There were a lot of places to eat down there. He parked near Ivar's and they made a quick walk across the street.

Once they were seated and had ordered some food, she rubbed her hands over her face wearily.

"You've had quite a day," he remarked.

"That's an understatement." She straightened and gave him a look. "You must be a masochist or something. First you keep coming back to the hospital to see the kids. Now you're inserting yourself in my problems—with my help, of course," she added, for the first time, cracking a smile.

He smiled back. "I told you before, the kids got to me. Occasionally, I follow up on someone I've crossed paths with on the job. It's nice to know how a story ends sometimes—especially if it's happy."

"I would imagine a lot of stories don't end happily."

"Some don't," he agreed. "But more do."

"I don't think I could do what you do. Risking my life for strangers." She shook her head, taking a sip of water. "It takes a certain kind of person to do that kind of thing."

"I grew up around firefighters. My dad was a battalion chief. I already told you about my brothers and sister. A few uncles dabbled in search and rescue, too. It's in my blood."

"That's neat," she said wistfully. "I mean the fact that you have a big family that seem close. After all this…" Her voice trailed off. "Sometimes I look back on things and have regrets. Especially now that my sister is gone."

"When was the last time you saw her?"

She stared out the window, her eyes clouded with emotion. "Thirteen years ago. She was fifteen."

"Wow."

"I graduated from high school and went off to college. She couldn't come with me." She still didn't look at him. "My parents were…difficult. I couldn't get away from them fast enough. My brother felt that way, too. He joined the Army—left years before I did. We had a weird childhood."

"I'm sorry."

She smiled halfway. "I'm sure my depressing story is really increasing your appetite. Let's change the subject."

"Okay," he agreed, sensing her discomfort. "You're a kindergarten teacher, right?"

"How did you know that?"

He hedged. He knew he shouldn't admit that Nick had given him personal information about her.

"Dr. Ryan?" she questioned.

He shook his head.

"Detective Holt," she figured out. She didn't seem angry.

"Don't get mad at Nick. He's really a pretty ethical guy. I basically wormed it out of him. It wasn't his fault. He's in a precarious place with my family right now because he and my sister are taking a break. We like to hold things over his head."

She chuckled at that. "Really. And why would you want to worm information out of him about me?"

He wasn't sure how to answer that question. It was definitely loaded. Giving up on beating around the bush, he looked her in the eye. "Honestly? You interest me."

Surprised, she frowned. "Me? Or the kids?"

"Both, I suppose."

They were quiet when the waiter set their meals down in front of them. They had both ordered fish and chips and the food looked delicious.

Casey picked up the ketchup and smothered his fries before he looked at her again. She was watching him curiously. "Did I make you uncomfortable?"

"I'm not sure what to think of you." She picked up a fry and nibbled on it. "You're different than anyone I've ever met. And that's odd for me to say because I hardly know you, yet I'm already certain of that fact."

"Is that a compliment?" he wondered, a little unsure how to read her.

"I wouldn't have said it if I'd meant it in a bad way." She leaned back against her seat. "Tell me about Nick and your sister. It's neutral ground. Somebody else's problems. It will get my mind off my own so I can eat."

He relaxed, digging into his food. "Colby's four years younger than me. She's the baby of the family and a bit spoiled." He chewed carefully. "Actually, she's more than a bit spoiled. Nick's got his hands full."

"I thought you said they're on a break."

"They've been on a break for the past year. I see them together all the time. It's one of those situations where they're in love—everyone knows it—but they just can't get their shit together."

"I don't know if that's romantic or tragic."

"It's both. They'll figure things out. I know my sister. She can't breathe without the guy. And he's the same way with her. Even when they're apart, he's got one eye on her, making sure she's safe." He wiped his mouth. "They've been together for three years—been pulling this on and off thing for one. As her family, we try to stay out of things but it can get hard sometimes."

"Because she's the baby," she figured out.

He shrugged and nodded. "And she's the

only girl. Three big brothers and a macho dad. Like I said, Nick's got his hands full."

She smiled at that.

He continued chewing his food, taking a moment to notice the way her face lit up when she was amused. "You've got a nice smile."

The smiled dimmed a little. "Are you really this charming or is this all an act?"

"It's not an act. I'm the most charming member of my family."

She shook her head at him but her smile brightened again.

"So what else do you want to talk about? There's only so much I can say about Colby and Nick."

"Tell me about your other brothers."

He thought that over. "Trent's the oldest. He's thirty-five, single and a little bit of a brooder. He keeps to himself. He just got promoted to lieutenant so he's been a bit of a pain lately. He outranks me and Brand now."

"Brandon was the one I met today," she recalled, finishing off her French fries.

"Yep. He's thirty—I'm thirty-two, by the way. There are two years between all of us but me and Trent. There's three years in between us."

"It's nice that you're all so close," she said again. "I can tell by the way you talk about your siblings that you really care about them."

"I do. I'd do anything for them."

She instantly tensed and he realized what he'd just said. "I wasn't trying to say anything negative about what you're doing, Aria. That came out wrong."

"No, I get it. I'm used to the disapproving frowns. The social worker at the hospital has been laying them on me for weeks. Dr. Ryan, while he's got a great poker face, has hit me with a few. Even Detective Holt thinks I'm a jerk for not quickly agreeing to take the kids home with me and raise them."

"I'm not giving you a disapproving frown." He straightened and tossed his napkin down on the table. "I get that this is a big deal. Kids don't raise themselves—at least they shouldn't have to. I can understand you being hesitant."

"Can you?" She turned to the window and stared out again.

"The fact that your sister gave you no warning of what was coming gives you a pass, Aria. She should have discussed this with you before she died—let you know what she was putting in her will."

"I know that. That's what I've been telling myself this whole time. But I'm still her sister. I know that's how everyone else is thinking, too. Maybe she didn't have any other option."

"That's possible," he agreed. "Or maybe she just knew deep down that you were the best person to raise the kids if something happened to her."

8

Aria studied Casey Gage for a long time. He was stumping her in more ways than one. First, he was honestly charming. He'd kept the conversation between them light and enjoyable. He was funny and charismatic. And honest. He cared about people, that much was obvious.

She found herself liking him a lot more than she wanted to.

"Did I say something wrong?" he asked, his brow arched.

"No," she replied instantly. "My sister didn't know me. Not the adult me that would be the one to raise her kids."

"Well, she picked you for some reason. I don't know if you'll ever know why."

She supposed that was one of the things that bothered her the most. The reasoning behind what her sister had done. "I do care about the kids." She wasn't sure why she was telling him this. After all, he hardly knew her. They would part ways after dinner and likely not see each other again—at least, not on such a personal level.

"I can see that. You wouldn't be running yourself ragged if you didn't."

She frowned at that. "You can tell I'm running myself ragged? Should I feel insulted?"

He gave her that irresistible grin again. "Not at all. You mentioned earlier this morning, when we ran into each other at the hospital, that you were mostly there visiting the kids at nights or on weekends because you were working."

She had told him that.

"You know, you could give it a try—taking Tiffany home when she's released. If it doesn't work out—"

She didn't let him finish. "If it doesn't work out, I can just take her back to social services, like one would return an unwanted piece of clothing to a department store."

He winced, clearly catching her sarcasm. "I see your point."

"The kids have been through enough. If I

take them home, it's a done deal. No matter what. I won't take them back. It *has* to work out." She looked him in the eye. "That's why I'm taking my time figuring things out. I *have* to be sure."

He was quiet for so long that she almost thought she'd offended him with her words. Then he spoke, catching her off guard. "I think I just figured out why your sister picked you."

The words were startling. But suddenly she understood what he meant.

"You care enough about them to be sure of what's best for *them*. That's all anyone would want for a guardian for their kids." He snatched the check when the waiter set it down on the table.

"What's my half?" she asked, digging into her purse.

"I've got it," he said, sliding his credit card into the slot in the leather billfold and setting it on the edge of the table for the waiter.

She attempted to grab it, but he stopped her.

She glanced down at their hands. His long fingers were wrapped around hers, not tightly, but firmly enough to stop her from moving. She looked into his face.

"I said, I've got it. It was my idea to eat. I'm paying." His hand lingered a moment longer before letting hers go.

She jerked her hand back, a little startled at

the reaction she had to his simple touch. Lord have mercy, she was attracted to him. More than attracted.

"It was just dinner, Aria. Don't look at me that way."

"What way?" she asked, resting her hands in her lap.

"You look like a deer sensing the crosshairs of a shotgun."

Did she?

She realized she might. She wasn't good with men, especially nice looking ones like this guy. She struggled to regain her composure. "I owe you a lot for what you've done—for the kids, for me. I should be buying your dinner."

"Do we have to go over the job thing again? It's getting old."

"Maybe pulling those kids out of the fire was your job. But doing all the other things you've done wasn't. I've wasted your whole day."

"Not hardly," was all he said, taking the bill from the waiter and scribbling on it before handing it back.

She wasn't sure how to respond to that. Was he telling her he'd enjoyed her company?

"We should get back to your car. Tow truck should be there by now." He slid his jacket on and climbed from the booth, waiting for her to follow him.

She did, silently. They walked back to his

truck, doing their best to thwart the rain drops beginning to fall.

When they arrived at her vehicle, they found the Triple A guy was already there. He quickly hooked her car up. She gave him the address of a nearby tire place. He was off a few minutes later.

She turned to Casey, who had stood behind her the entire time, waiting patiently. "I really can get a cab from here. I need to pick out some tires. Then I plan to stop in at the hospital. But I appreciate the time you've taken helping me out. I enjoyed dinner. It was...nice." She smiled up at him.

He shoved his hands into the pockets of his jeans. "Yeah, it was. But I'm not letting you take a cab. Are you going to hold out on me for a long time arguing about that? Because if you are, I think we should probably move inside the fire station and out of this rain."

The serious look on his face told her he wasn't going to back down. "You *are* a masochist," was all she finally said.

He motioned for her to follow him to his truck. Once they were back inside, he shot her a sidelong glance. "For the record, Aria, I don't consider hanging out with you painful."

The words successfully silenced her.

He drove her to the nearby tire center, where she picked out four new tires that the sales clerk assured her would be installed by the following afternoon. After that, they headed for the hospital. It was after seven so traffic was a bit lighter than it had been earlier. They were even able to park without a problem.

The moment they entered the hospital, Casey was greeted by several people. A nurse here, a doctor there. Aria didn't miss the interested looks that were tossed his way—the arched brows—when the people noticed she was walking with him. He didn't seem to realize the curiosity that surrounded them. Either that, or he plain didn't care.

She stepped into the elevator and he followed, pushing the button to the third floor. The ride was brisk. At this time of the evening, the waiting room was quiet, all the televisions on low. They passed the nurses station and continued down the hall to the room Tiffany and Jaden had been moved to.

The moment Aria went around the corner, she sensed something was off. It was the smell...gardenias. Someone's perfume.

Her heart stopped. She knew that scent— had smelled it every day of her life up until she was seventeen years old.

Her eyes peered into the room, praying her imagination was getting the better of her.

But it wasn't. Adele Carlisle was seated in the chair next to Tiffany's bed, rolling yarn into a ball, as though it were the most natural place for her to be.

For a minute, Aria couldn't speak. Her voice felt frozen. Hell, her entire brain felt frozen.

"Hello, Aria."

Her mother's voice sounded different—scratchy, older. Her face looked different, too. She had lines around her green eyes—green eyes that were nearly identical to the ones Aria possessed—the ones her sister had possessed as well. Lyla's daughter had those same eyes, too.

Adele was in decent physical shape. Slim and trim. Her once dark hair had grayed at the temples and spottily throughout, but she appeared healthy. Far healthier than she had thirteen years earlier.

"Maybe I should wait outside," Casey said, reminding her that he was standing right behind her.

"No, don't run off on my account." Adele jumped to her feet and walked toward him, her hand held out politely. "I'm Adele Carlisle. Aria's mother."

Casey shook her hand politely. "Casey Gage."

"What are you doing here?" Aria finally found her voice to demand. She knew the words came out coldly and she couldn't make herself feel any remorse.

"What do you mean, what am I doing here?"

Adele frowned. "These are my grandchildren. I'm here to help."

"Help what?" Aria asked carefully.

"I'll give you two a minute," Casey said, more forcefully this time. He was already backing up into the hallway. He looked at Aria. "I'll be in the waiting room when you're done here." He was gone a moment later.

Aria rounded on her mother. "You're here because you spoke with the police."

"Naturally. Lyla was my daughter."

Aria really had no way of knowing how close Lyla had remained to their mother over the years. Evidently she'd had some type of relationship with the woman.

"You are the one who disappeared from our lives, Aria Jane. Not me," Adele snapped, shooting Aria a lethal look. "Now I would appreciate it if you wouldn't come in here and upset the children. They've been through enough, don't you think?"

Aria glanced at Tiffany first. She was sleeping soundly. There was an empty dinner tray on her table.

"I fed her. She was quite happy to see me," Adele announced, stepping back and sitting in the chair again. "Jaden's still the same. But he was blinking earlier and making some noises. There was a young doctor in here that seemed hopeful he's going to wake up soon."

Aria felt a pang of regret for the fact that she'd missed Dr. Ryan when he'd come through on his rounds. She shut her eyes and took a minute to get herself under control. The truth was, this wasn't about her. It was beginning to look as though Lyla had had a relationship with Adele—and likely her children had, too.

For some reason that fact didn't fill Aria with relief like it should have. She wasn't alone in this anymore. The children now had another alternative. So why didn't she feel better about things?

She reminded herself that Lyla hadn't mentioned a word about Adele in her will. That was an interesting fact.

"Stop standing there looking at me like I'm the devil. You always were dramatic."

"I was never dramatic, Mother," Aria said tightly. "You realize that Lyla has left me in charge of the children." Here she was, pointing out a fact that she'd been trying to dispute for two weeks now. She wasn't sure why. Except that the very sight of her mother set her teeth on edge.

"I'm aware of that fact." Adele's expression turned cold. "I was told by the police that you aren't willing to take responsibility for the children. The social worker that was in here earlier reiterated the same thing to me."

Aria felt her skin grow hot. "I haven't made

any such decision. Not officially."

Adele rolled her eyes. "Leave it to you to make this about yourself. These poor babies have been through hell, Aria. They need stability, not some stranger that can't decide whether she wants to help them or not."

Anger washed over Aria and she bit back the retort she had on the tip of her tongue that she knew wouldn't help the situation. "I'm aware of what the children need. I've been here by their bedsides for two weeks now."

"I would have been here, too, if you had bothered to call me," Adele said indignantly.

When Tiffany rolled over in her sleep and let out a moan, Aria was reminded of the fact that she could hear every word they were saying. She shot Adele a look. "We're not going to talk any more about this right now."

Adele rolled her eyes a second time, but sat back down in the chair.

Aria wasn't sure what to think of this version of her mother. She seemed nothing like the alcoholic, abusive monster that Aria had grown up with.

"I have a right to be here," Adele said petulantly. "I'm a blood relative. There's nothing you can do about that."

Adele was right. There was nothing Aria could do about her presence. But there was no way in hell she was going to sit here with the woman. It would only cause more tension and stress in the room, which would be worse for the children. "I'm going to go home. I'll be back in the morning."

"Suit yourself," was all Adele said. She went back to rolling her ball of yarn.

Aria gave the kids each one last glance, then stepped out into the hallway. She took a moment before heading for the waiting room. There was no way she was letting Casey Gage see her in the condition she was in. When she was sure she was relatively put back together, she walked down the hallway.

Casey was seated in a corner chair, his ankles crossed. The television in the corner had his full attention until she cleared her throat. Then his gaze turned her way. He gave her a sympathetic smile. "Ready?"

"Yes, thanks."

He stood and they made their way back downstairs and into the parking garage. He didn't speak until they were on the road and headed toward her neighborhood. "You okay?"

She really didn't want to answer that question. Her mind was jumbled right now. She felt a myriad of different emotions—none of which were good. "I'm okay," she forced out.

He nodded, appearing to accept her answer.

"That was my mother," she said, knowing he

deserved some type of explanation for the surreal situation.

"She mentioned that—and you resemble her a little."

She scowled before she could stop herself.

"You can't choose your parents," was all he said.

"Don't I know it," she muttered, and turned to stare out the window.

"So I realize you have issues with her. But she's here for the kids. That's a good thing, right?"

She wished she knew how to answer that question, but she didn't. Her mother had always been a complicated individual. Her presence at the hospital was a jarring reminder of that reality.

"You've had a long day. Maybe after you sleep on things, you'll be able to make more sense out of this."

"There is no making sense out of my mother."

"Family can be complicated," he agreed. "She didn't seem unhappy to see you."

"No," she agreed. "But she didn't have a whole lot of kind things to say after you stepped out of the room."

"I'm guessing you didn't, either."

She scowled at him again, this time a little annoyed with his honest take on things. "You hardly know me, Casey."

He instantly backed off. "That's true. I'm sorry."

She wasn't sure why she was taking her anger out on him. He was only speaking the truth. He'd seen what he'd seen. "I can't be nice to her."

"Okay. I'm not judging you."

"Everyone is judging me right now, thanks to my sister."

He pulled to a stop in front of the address she'd given him. "Nice neighborhood," he mused, ignoring her comment.

Her house sat on a nicely manicured street in a middle-class neighborhood. It was one story, with a nice sized backyard. She'd fallen in love with it the moment she'd seen it. Over the years, she'd thought about buying it, but the owner wasn't interested in selling so far.

"I like it. I've lived here for six years now — ever since I got my first teaching job." She grabbed her purse and reached for the door handle, anxious to let him be on his way. She'd already taken up way more of his time than was reasonable. "Thank you for everything. I'm sorry for..." Her voice trailed off. "I didn't expect to find my mother at the hospital tonight."

"I figured," he said, resting an arm on the steering wheel. "You want me to walk you up?"

"The porch is twenty feet away," she said, giving him a small smile.

He shrugged. "Twenty feet is twenty feet."

"I'll be fine," she assured him and opened the door. She hopped down, giving him one last look. "Thank you for dinner."

"You're welcome."

She felt like she owed him something more, after everything he'd done for her. "I appreciate you helping me out. I guess I should have gotten you more than one box of those cookies, huh?"

He chuckled at that. "Bakery's open tomorrow. I'm always hungry."

She found herself grinning. She let the door shut and walked up to her porch, quickly shoving her key in the lock. He waited until she was safely inside the house before he put the truck in gear and drove off down the street.

9

Casey parked his truck at the curb. He noticed right away that Kaylee's Prius wasn't the only vehicle in his driveway. She had company. The idea that she had a man in the house crossed his mind. Maybe she'd finally accepted that he wasn't interested in her. Maybe she was finally going to move on.

His mood brightened and he contemplated the situation. He didn't really relish the idea of walking in on them in action — not because he was jealous — but because of the awkward position interrupting them would put him in.

He started up his truck again and headed to his sister's place.

Colby lived in a brownstone on the outskirts

of downtown. Her apartment was on the fifth floor of a well-maintained building. The two-bedroom had been updated with new appliances and carpeting. She had nice view of the city lights. He liked the place. And once in a while he crashed in her spare bedroom. Tonight was going to be one of those times.

He thought about calling her, then changed his mind. He was already turning onto her block. He knew she wasn't working tomorrow because they worked the same schedule.

Five minutes later, he was knocking on her door. He didn't get any response for several moments. After he knocked one more time, he finally heard shuffling from inside the apartment. Then he heard her mutter a curse.

"I heard that," he said, giving her a look through the peephole.

She opened the door a second later. He instantly realized what had taken her so long. She was in her bathrobe. Her hair was mussed. Clearly she'd been sleeping.

"Shit. Sorry. I guess I should have called."

She rolled her eyes. "Every time I try to go to bed early…" She held the door open so he could come inside. "Let me guess, Kaylee's home tonight."

"She is," he confirmed, stepping into the apartment. He took a quick glance around, making sure she was alone.

"What are you doing?"

"Looking for Nick."

She rolled her eyes. "He's not here, Casey. We're broken up. Do you not understand what that means?"

He folded his arms over his chest and met her gaze. "With you two? It means you still hook up every ten minutes for a quickie."

She glowered at him. "Quickie? Really?"

"It is what it is. This wouldn't be the first time I've interrupted you guys during one of your *break ups*."

She let the door shut behind him. "I'm not sure how much clearer I can make this for you. We are not together. We're not even speaking, let alone having sex."

He winced at the words. "Thanks for sharing."

"You're the one who brought it up."

"Okay, okay," he relented.

"You want a beer?"

"Sure." He leaned against the counter as she stalked into the kitchen and pulled out two beers. She popped the tops and offered him one.

"So what's on your mind?"

He took a long swallow. "Nothing. I told you, Kaylee's at the house."

She gave him a knowing look. "You'd be at Trent's right now if you were just looking for a place to crash."

He supposed she was right about that. Trent was a man of few words for the most part. When Casey was in the mood to talk, he generally went to his sister. "I think Kaylee's got a guy at the house."

Colby frowned, her beer poised at her lips. "A guy? What the hell!"

"I'm not unhappy about it," Casey said quickly, making sure he made himself clear. "It's a good thing."

"You don't take women to the house. You told me that yourself. Why does she get to have men there?"

He supposed he should be annoyed but he wasn't. He was so damned hopeful that his ex was moving on that he couldn't muster up any irritation. "Maybe she'll fall in love with the asshole and run off with him. Then I can have my house back."

"Wishful thinking on your part." She walked over and sat down on the couch. "So I heard that the kids' aunt came by the station today."

"Who told you that?" Of course he already knew who. Brandon. His little brother always had been a big mouth.

"Don't play dumb with me. I was told she gave you cookies. And that she's hot."

"She gave me cookies," he confirmed. He

didn't touch the *hot* comment—even if he did agree.

"So she's *not* hot?"

"I didn't say that." He reached for the remote to the television. She grabbed it out of his hand and gave him a look.

"Spill."

"Spill what?"

"You're into her."

Again, he remained silent.

"Ha! Finally! I'm so happy!"

He rolled his eyes. "About what? So I think she's cute. Big deal."

"Cute, or hot?" she asked, leaning back against the couch.

"Does it matter?"

"Yes, it does. Cute is endearing. Hot is sexy."

He resisted the urge to roll his eyes again. "I hardly know her, Colby. We went out to dinner one time." He wanted the words back as soon as they left his mouth. "It wasn't a date," he quickly added.

"You went out with her?" Colby didn't bother hiding her excitement. "Unbelievable. So tell me what happened."

"Nothing happened. And it wasn't like that—like a date."

"Did you drive there together?"

He shrugged and nodded. "Her tires were

slashed. She couldn't drive."

"Did you have a nice conversation that resulted in a little flirting and a whole lot of smiling?"

He knew he should deny it, but he didn't. He nodded again.

"Did you pay?"

"Oh for cryin' out loud!"

"You did! I knew it! It was a date!"

"A date is when a guy asks a girl out, picks her up at her place, and they go to a planned event together. This wasn't planned. We were killing time until a tow truck showed up."

"You're downplaying. That's okay. I can tell you like her. What's she like?"

There were times when he wanted to strangle his sister, even if he did love her to pieces. "I don't know. She's nice. There's more to her than meets the eye."

"Meaning?"

"Meaning, she's not as bad as everyone's making her out to be. She cares about those kids. That's most of the reason she hasn't committed to taking responsibility for them."

Colby thought that over. "Well, they are her kin. Who else do they have?"

He thought about Adele Carlisle. "Maybe Aria's mother. I drove her by to see the kids before I took her home—and before you ask, no I did not go into her house."

Colby snickered. "I wasn't going to ask you that."

"Yes, you were. Anyway, her mother was at the hospital. Their relationship is strained, to say the least. But the woman seems interested in the kids." He finished off his beer.

His sister was just staring at him, a grin on her face. He could tell she was still stuck on the fact that he'd had dinner with Aria.

"Just reel in your antennas. There's no story here." At least not yet, he added to himself.

"It's early. Time will tell."

He refused to give her any more fodder. "I'm tired. Since Detective Hottie's not here, can I crash in your spare room tonight?"

She made a face at the nickname Nick had been pinned with by her girlfriends early on in their relationship. "You need to stop talking about him."

"Why? He'll be back in a week or two. He always is."

The smile that had been on her face earlier quickly evaporated. She didn't seem sad really—Colby wasn't one for emotions. She did look a little worried. "Okay. What's wrong?"

She shrugged her shoulders. "Nothing's wrong. I just don't like to think about him."

"Not thinking about him doesn't make him any less real."

"Duh," she snapped, getting up and heading

into the kitchen. "I guess it just makes me miss him a little, that's all."

He watched as she poured what was left of her beer down the sink. "That's a waste of good alcohol."

"You want it, go after it." She tossed her bottle into the trash.

"If you're miserable without him, why don't you try and fix things?"

"I already told you, I saw him with another girl."

"I'm telling you, you overreacted to that. She was a co-worker."

"So he says."

"He's not much for lying," he reminded her.

She shrugged her shoulders, looking a little forlorn.

Immediately Casey felt pity for her, even though he knew she was her own worst enemy. He didn't like seeing his little sister unhappy. He stood up, setting his empty bottle on the counter. "You want me to be honest with you, or be your coddling big brother?"

She appeared conflicted. Finally she muttered a curse. "Honest, I guess."

"I'm not going to sugarcoat this so brace yourself." He gave her a sharp look. "Quit playing games with Nick. He's a good guy. He loves you. Right now, he's willing to take from you what he can get. He's a good looking guy with a lot of female attention. Sooner or later, he's going to get tired of your shit and cut you loose for good. I don't think you want that, do you?"

She exhaled, running a hand through her hair. "Maybe you should have been the coddling big brother."

He shook his head, reaching over and giving her the hug he knew she needed, yet would never ask for. "I've never been in love like you and Nick are. That being said, you're a couple of train wrecks. Fix things."

She accepted his hug, tucking her head underneath his chin. "He's really angry with me. I said some rotten things to him."

"You?" He feigned surprise.

She backed up and slugged him in the arm. "I can't help my hot Irish temper. It comes from Mom's side of the family."

"Blame it on whoever you want." He set her away from him and reached for his cell phone. "You got an extra charger around here?"

She reached into a drawer and pulled one out. "So are you going to call the aunt?—maybe ask her out on a real date?"

"Worry about yourself, little sister. You've got plenty of problems of your own." He gave her nose a tweak and headed for the spare bedroom.

10

Aria awoke from a sound sleep to her cell phone ringing. It took her a moment before she was coherent enough to reach over to the bedside table, where the device was plugged in.

She glanced at the screen. The call was unknown. She answered it, knowing that sometimes calls from the hospital showed up that way on her phone.

"Ms. Carlisle? This is Chloe Chastain. I'm a nurse here at Seattle General Pediatric."

"Yes?" Aria responded, suddenly wide awake. Immediately her imagination started running wild. Something had happened to the kids.

"I'm sorry to bother you in the middle of the

night. We had an incident with your niece earlier. She's extremely upset right now. We can give her a sedative, but I thought I should call you before we do."

Aria sat up straight. "What happened?"

"I'm not entirely sure. I just know she was screaming when I walked into the room. Now she's in there terrified, claiming someone was in the room besides her brother—who is still not responsive, by the way."

"Is my mother there?"

"No, ma'am. There's nobody in the room. I did a solid check. I think she may have had a nightmare. But she's scared and alone…" The nurse paused. "I know you've been spending a lot of time with her. I just thought maybe you'd want to be with her—considering what she's been through and all."

Aria slid her legs over the side of the bed. "Don't sedate her just yet if you can help it. I'll be there as soon as I can." She hung up her phone and dressed quickly. She didn't remember she didn't have a car until she dug into her purse for her keys and found them missing.

"Damn it!"

She dragged the phone book out and looked up the number for a twenty-four-hour cab service. Forty minutes later, she was on her way down the hall to her niece's room. When she walked through the door, she saw that Tiffany wasn't alone. There was a nurse with her, sitting in the chair beside her bed.

When Tiffany saw Aria, she started to cry again.

The nurse gave Aria a helpless frown and stood up, moving so Aria could take her place.

"It's okay, Tiffany. You're safe," Aria said, setting her purse down and sitting on the side of the child's bed.

"He's going to come back. He wants to hurt me."

Aria could see the fear in the child's eyes. "You were dreaming, sweetie. See? There's nobody here but you and me and Jaden and the nurse. You're safe."

Tiffany shook her head adamantly. "I want to go home! I hate it here! And Jaden's not going to wake up! He's going to die, just like Mommy and just like Daddy!"

Aria felt her heart breaking for the child. "I'm sorry. I wish I could make this easier for you."

Tiffany continued to cry. When Aria tried to comfort her, she pulled away, burrowing into her blankets.

"Dr. Ryan okay'd a sedative," the nurse said, giving Aria a sympathetic look. "I think maybe it would be best at this point."

Aria nodded, slowly backing away while the

nurse reached for Tiffany's IV and went to work administering the medicine. A few minutes later, all was quiet. Tiffany had finally fallen asleep.

"I'm sorry I dragged you down here. I just thought…" The nurse shrugged sheepishly. "She was so frightened."

"It's fine," Aria said, setting her purse on the table next to the bed. "I'm going to stay if you don't mind."

The nurse smiled. "Certainly. I'll be out at the desk if you need me."

Aria slid into the chair between the kids' beds and made herself comfortable. She watched for a long time as Tiffany slept. Something in the little girl's eyes as she'd cried had penetrated its way into Aria's soul. Her fear was very real, dream or not. Someone was haunting her nightmares. But who?

"Aunt Aria?"

Aria wasn't sure where the words came from at first. She looked at Tiffany but the child was snoring softly. Knowing there was nobody else in the room but Jaden, she turned and glanced at his bed. The little boy was lying there, his eyes wide open.

Aria stood up immediately, hurrying across the room to his bed. He stared up at her, his big brown eyes filled with the same terror she'd seen in his sister's minutes earlier. "You called me Aunt Aria. You know who I am?"

"You're Mommy's sister. I heard Tiffy call you that."

His voice was soft and scratchy, probably from lack of use.

She reached behind him for the call button. His voice stopped her before she completed the task. "Tiffy's not lying. It wasn't a dream. There was someone in here. A bad, bad man. And he's going to come back."

. . .

Aria sipped her coffee. She was in the waiting room now. She had been for the last hour. After the nurses had come into the room and realized Jaden was awake, the on call physician had been summoned to the room. They'd been running a battery of tests on the little boy ever since, which so far had all come back excellent.

While she was waiting, Aria had contemplated what her nephew had told her. He was a six-year-old. A traumatized six-year-old. He'd been asleep for two weeks. It was possible that he'd imagined the entire scenario he'd described earlier. But the fact that his sister had described the same exact thing was concerning. So she'd dug through her purse, finally coming across the card that Nick Holt had given her, and called the detective. He'd been asleep, naturally. It was just after six in the morning on a Sunday. But he'd assured her he was on his way.

Fortunately, she didn't have to wait long for him to show up. He walked out of the elevator not twenty minutes later. He was dressed casually this time, in jeans and a t-shirt, but his gun and badge were still clipped to his belt. He caught sight of her immediately and joined her in the waiting room, taking the empty chair beside her.

"I'm sorry I woke you up," she said quietly. "I wasn't sure whether I should or not, but..." Her voice trailed off.

"You did the right thing. How is he?"

"His tests are coming back good. Doctor's hopeful. They're still not finished. That's why I'm out here."

"So, tell me again what happened."

She thought back to the events of the night before. After relaying everything that had gone on with the children, she waited for him to give his take on things.

"They both described exactly the same thing?"

She nodded. "Pretty much. Jaden swears there was someone in the room. A bad, bad man." The words made her shiver. "I know the nurse didn't see anyone. She says Tiffany had to have been dreaming. But both of the kids seemed terrified."

"And then Jaden just woke up? Out of nowhere?"

She shrugged, clasping her coffee cup tightly in her hands. "That's the way it looked to me. But it's possible he's been conscious for longer than we think. I told you what Dr. Ryan said about him having a mental reason to stay asleep."

Holt nodded. "Okay. Well I need to speak with the kids when the doctors say it's okay. I'll wait as long as it takes. I'd like to do it sooner rather than later."

"I figured. That's why I called you." She stared down at the floor, another matter on her mind all together. "I should let you know, my mother's here."

"Here in the hospital?"

"Not right now, but she was last night. When I came back here, after getting my car towed, I found her sitting by Tiffany's bed." She blew out a breath, wishing she could expel the memory from her brain.

"Okay. Maybe she was in the room last night. Maybe the kids didn't realize it was her."

"I thought about that. I asked the nurse. She said nobody was in there. I don't know when my mother left the hospital, but I left shortly after eight. She was still here then and looked pretty comfortable."

"Meaning you don't think she was planning on going anywhere anytime soon," he figured out.

"No." She straightened, shutting her eyes for a moment. "I can't give you any information about Adele Carlisle, Detective. I hardly know her myself anymore. I have no idea where she's staying, or what she's up to. She told me she's here for the children. She acts as if she has a relationship with them."

"Did you ask Tiffany about that?"

"I didn't get the chance. She was terrified last night—not making any sense. Then the nurse sedated her." She met his gaze. "She looks different than I remember. My mother, I mean. I don't know if that's a good thing or a bad thing."

His expression turned sympathetic. "Okay. I appreciate your honesty. Maybe you should go home and get some sleep. You look like you could use it."

She had no intention of leaving the kids on their own again. She didn't tell him that. "What if what they saw was real?"

He frowned at that. "Chances are, it wasn't. They've been through an awful lot over the past two weeks. Sometimes PTSD hits and what you see seems very real."

"But what if it *was* real?"

He let out a sigh. "I can't determine that

without talking to the kids myself. But if I think there's reason, I'll put an officer on their door."

Satisfied with that, she nodded.

"I'm going to go check on the situation. You really should go home and get some sleep."

She nodded absently, not really comfortable with that idea at all.

He got up and disappeared down the hallway.

She curled up in her chair, finally giving into the feeling of exhaustion that had been threatening her for days. Her eyes slid shut and a moment later she drifted off to sleep.

11

Casey walked into the hospital just after ten that morning. Nick had called him—told him about the events of the night before. He had the idea in his head that Casey had *something* going with Aria. Something personal. Casey hadn't bothered correcting him. He'd been more concerned about what had happened with the kids during the night. Nick wasn't positive that the children had actually seen a dangerous man in their room. All the same, he'd decided to stick an officer on their door for the remainder of their stay in the hospital.

Casey figured that was a good idea. Better to be safe than sorry.

He started to head down the hallway toward

the room the kids were in when he saw Aria. He was a little surprised to see her curled up in a waiting room chair, sound asleep.

"She's been there off and on for hours."

Casey turned. Alex walked up. He was wearing jeans today, rather than his normal scrubs. He indicated Aria. "She should go home. The grandmother's in there with the kids. I'm getting the feeling that there's no love lost between her and her daughter."

Casey didn't deny the obvious. "So what's the deal with things?"

Alex shrugged. "There's a cop on the door—Nick's doing. He spoke with both kids. They stuck to their story."

"Yeah, I heard about that. Do you think they really saw someone in the room last night?"

Alex folded his arms over his chest. "It's possible. There's always activity going on in the hospital—even in the middle of the night. But I'm doubting it was a dangerous man, threatening to hurt them. It was likely a nurse or doctor doing rounds. After what the kids witnessed the night of that fire, it would be no wonder if their having flashbacks and getting confused." Alex nodded over at Aria again. "You got a thing with her?"

Casey frowned. "I hardly know her."

"Rumor has it she was in here with you last night. Now you're back again. She was at the firehouse." Alex grinned. "Word travels."

Casey muttered an oath. "Just don't worry about it."

"I was only hitting you up because I thought about asking her out. But if you're—"

"I am," Casey said, leaving nothing left to discuss.

Alex chuckled. "I thought so. I figured it didn't hurt to ask."

Casey just scowled.

"Easy, boy. It's all good. I have rounds. I'll see you later." Alex was gone a moment later.

Casey couldn't seem to wipe the scowl off his face for a full minute. He wasn't sure why he was so annoyed. After all, he'd had one meal with Aria Carlisle. They barely knew each other.

But he wanted to know more.

The idea irritated him further. It had been so long since he'd liked a woman enough to take a chance on her, that he almost didn't know what to do about the situation.

He looked over at her again. She seemed small and defenseless, curled up in that waiting room chair all alone. That got to him even more—the fact that she was alone. She'd been tossed into this nightmare, with nobody at her side.

Rubbing a hand over his chin, he sighed in resignation. He was going to have to go for broke. Either that or walk away. And he realized he didn't want to walk away.

He strode into the waiting room. There were a few people scattered about, some on their phones, others watching the morning news. Nobody paid him any attention.

He sat down in the chair next to hers and waited patiently. He figured it was probably better to let her get some sleep. He had nothing planned for the day. It was Sunday, usually his lazy day. He leaned back and settled in for the long haul.

. . .

When Aria's eyes flickered open, it took her a moment to remember where she was. The hospital. In the waiting room. Her mother had shown up, and she'd been afraid to leave the kids by themselves — even with a police officer outside the door. So she'd gone back to her ever faithful waiting room chair and curled into it. When she'd closed her eyes, she'd been alone. She realized now, that she wasn't.

Sitting up straight, she looked at Casey, confused. He was just sitting there next to her, his long legs stretched out in front of him, his arms crossed over his chest as he watched her carefully. Now that he saw she was awake, he grinned at her.

"Good morning."

"What are you doing here?" she said in response.

"Waiting for you to wake up. Nick called me."

Nick. Detective Holt, she reminded herself. "Why would he call you?"

He straightened. "Because he thought I'd want to know what happened last night with the kids—which I did, by the way—want to know, I mean."

"Oh." She relaxed a little. She supposed he did have a vested interest in the kids. He'd been checking on them for weeks.

"I've been told to take you home."

She uncurled her legs and stretched them out. Then she considered him. "By who?"

"Dr. Ryan, for one. Nick, for another. They think you should go and get some sleep at home. I think they're probably right."

"I don't care what anyone thinks. I'm not leaving those kids alone."

"There's a cop on the door, Aria. And your mother's in there with them right now."

She scowled at that.

"Listen, I'm just trying to help. If you can sleep that soundly in a waiting room chair, your body is trying to tell you something. You're going to hit bottom. You won't be much help to anyone then."

"Didn't you and I just meet yesterday?" she

asked irritably.

"Technically, yes."

"Then why does it feel like we've known each other for so much longer?"

He grinned. "I was thinking the same thing."

"That wasn't a compliment." She climbed to her feet.

"It kind of was." He followed suit, still grinning.

If he hadn't looked so appealing, she would have been much more annoyed. Instead, she found herself admiring the firm shape of his jaw—the thick layer of stubble there. She'd never been much of a stubble girl, but on him it was— She stopped herself. *Nothing*. It was nothing. *He* was nothing. She had bigger problems to deal with at this point. Her mother, for one. She needed to talk to the kids and get to the bottom of their relationship with Adele. Did they really know her as well as she claimed they did?

"I can wait here for you if you want to go talk to the kids. Then I'll take you to pick up your car." He sat back down in his chair, turning his attention to the television.

"Casey?"

He glanced at her.

"Why are you doing this? You hardly know me."

"I thought we talked about this last night. I told you, you interest me."

She was at a loss for words again.

"I don't mean to be rude, but the clock is ticking. Maybe I have something better to do today."

"What if I tell you that you don't interest me?"

"I think you'd be lying. Go ahead and do your thing, sweetheart. I'll be here waiting when you're done."

Frustrated, she scowled at him. How could he be so incorrigible and so…*hot*…all at the same time?

Figuring there was no point in arguing with him, she headed down the hallway. Just as she rounded the corner, she caught sight of the uniformed officer sitting in a chair outside the kids' room. He was doing something on his cell phone. When he saw her, he smiled. "How's it going?"

"Good," she replied. She glanced into the room, prepared to ask her mother to beat it for a few minutes so she could talk to the kids alone. What she saw made her stop dead in her tracks. Adele was on the bed with Jaden. Tiffany had joined them. They were all cuddled together, reading a book. Adele was chirping like a bird and making all kinds of other animal sounds. And the kids appeared as comfortable as all get out. They were snuggled into her side, looking at the pictures on each page.

Taken aback, Aria stood there stupidly.

"You can come in if you want," Adele said, not looking away from the pages.

Both kids peered up at Aria. Neither said a word.

Feeling like a third wheel, Aria shook her head, suddenly changing her mind about approaching the kids. Clearly they did have a relationship with their grandmother, as hard as that was for Aria to comprehend. "I just wanted to tell you, I'm going to go home and take a shower. I'll be back later."

"Take your time," was all Adele said.

Aria stared a moment longer, still shocked by what she was seeing. She could remember a time, very, very long ago, when her mother had read stories to her—to Lyla. Even to Michael. And then the drinking had started.

"Come in or go out. Don't stand there and stare," Adele complained, giving Aria an exasperated look.

"I'm going," Aria said, and walked out of the room. She found Casey in the waiting room, right where she'd left him.

"That was fast," he remarked, hauling himself to his feet.

She followed him silently out to his truck. He started it up and headed toward the tire place without being told to.

"Are you going to yell at me if I ask you what you're upset about?"

She shook her head. "I'm not upset. Not really."

He waited for her to say more.

"I feel like I'm being punk'd."

The words hung in the air for a moment.

"Your mother's not what you expected," he translated, although she wasn't sure how. She knew she wasn't making much sense.

"No, she's not." She bit her bottom lip thoughtfully. "I was going to ask the kids about her. But they were all cuddled together in bed reading. She was making animal sounds."

"That doesn't seem like a bad thing," he said carefully.

"It wouldn't be. It *shouldn't* be. I don't know." She ran a hand through her hair. "I'm so tired I think my brain is short circuiting."

"I told you, you need some sleep."

"I can't sleep. I'll go home and lie there for hours. Then I'll get back up and head to the hospital. It's what I do almost every night. Except for last night when I actually did fall asleep and then the hospital called and woke me up."

He slanted her a sympathetic look. "Stress will do that to you sometimes. You need a stress reliever."

"Like what?" she asked curiously.

"I can think of a few things."

She heard the undertone in his voice and gave him a startled look. "Are you flirting again? I'm so tired I can't tell."

"Do you want me to flirt with you?" He kept his eyes on the road.

Did she? She gave him another once over. His hair was tousled, either from the wind outside or from his fingers raking through it, which she'd seen him do numerous times over the past twenty-four hours. The tousled look was good on him. He was tough looking, not sloppy. The t-shirt he wore fit him snugly in all the right places. So did his jeans.

Yes, she decided. She did want him to flirt with her. But she wasn't about to tell him that.

He pulled up in front of the tire shop and came to a stop. He didn't bother turning off the engine. "I guess I'll see you."

She raised a brow. A minute ago he'd been flirting with her, now he was talking to her with all of the feeling a person used when talking to a dead fish. What the hell?

"What?" he asked, his own brow curved.

"Nothing." She reached for the door handle.

He leaned over, his fingers gripping the skin of her upper arm. He gave her a tug and she turned, their gazes colliding. The next thing she knew, his mouth was on hers, hot and full of promise. She felt his tongue dart against her lips once then twice before gaining the entrance it was after. And then she was lost. She dropped her purse onto the floor of his truck in her haste to get closer to him.

His fingers reached up and cupped her jaw, tilting her head back to give him better access. Then he kissed her again, this time without preliminaries. Their tongues swirled together erotically until she felt like she couldn't breathe.

God, he tasted good. Like coffee and peppermint. And he smelled good too. Citrusy, with a hint of pine.

"Get your car." He spoke the words softly against her mouth. "And then follow me to my house."

Breathing hard, she looked into his eyes. "I can't."

"You can." He kissed her again, his teeth taking the time to nibble on her bottom lip.

She was nibbling back before she realized it. Not only that, she'd damn near slid into his lap. She pulled back, struggling for breath. "We hardly know each other."

"I know enough." He brushed a lock of hair out of her face.

She had never been one to take sex lightly. She'd had two serious relationships in her life — both of which had ended badly. So why was she actually contemplating sleeping with a man she'd only known for two days?

He leaned down, rubbed his nose against hers. "Just follow me. If you get there and decide you don't want to do anything, that's okay. We'll just talk."

The words surprised her. "You're inviting me to your house to talk?"

He gave her a knowing look. "Absolutely not. But if that's what you want to do, I'm game. I just want to spend some time with you."

She felt herself caving. She wanted to spend some time with him, too. But not talking. That was what scared her.

"I'll wait for you," he urged, giving her a nod. "My place is five minutes from here."

Her head nodded before her brain thought things through.

He reached over and got the door for her, giving it a shove.

She picked up her purse and climbed from the vehicle before she changed her mind.

12

Casey waited out in front of the tire shop for ten minutes, contemplating what he'd just done. He'd invited Aria to his house—the house he shared with his ex-fiancé.

And he felt good about it. For the first time in a year, he didn't give a rip what Kaylee thought about him bringing a woman home. She was the one that was choosing to stay where she wasn't wanted.

On the other hand, Aria wasn't likely to understand the situation. He was going to have to explain it.

He frowned at that and thought about telling her they should go to her place.

She stepped out of the tire shop at that

moment, her keys in her hand. She glanced up at him, her eyes locking with his.

Was she going to chicken out?

He waited to see if she'd walk toward his truck. She surprised him by climbing into her car and starting it up.

He took a deep breath. He could go to her right now and explain the situation—give her an out. But he didn't want to. Even if they didn't end up in bed when they got to his house, he didn't care. He really did just want to spend time with her.

He threw his truck into gear and drove out of the parking lot. He watched her follow in his rearview mirror.

When they pulled up in front of his house five minutes later, he was relieved to see that Kaylee's car wasn't parked in the driveway.

He quickly shut off his truck. By the time Aria pulled up and parked, he was leaning against his rig, watching her.

She climbed from her car and walked up the driveway, her hands in the pockets of her jeans. She considered him. "Nice house."

"Thanks." He gestured for her to follow him up the walk.

She hesitated. "I don't know if this is such a good idea."

He nodded toward the house. "We don't have to do anything you don't want to do."

"That's the problem. I do want to do…" Her voice trailed off. "I don't sleep around, Casey. It's not in my nature."

He frowned at that. "Neither do I, believe it or not."

She stayed rooted where she was. "I should really get back to the hospital."

He walked over and looked down at her. "Come in and have a beer or something. No big deal."

"I should get back to the hospital," she repeated.

"Your mother's there," he reminded her. "The kids aren't alone."

She blew out a breath. "Even so…"

"Just come in for a few minutes. Like I said, we can talk."

"Just talk?"

"If that's what you want." He reached for her hand.

She let him take it after a moment.

A few minutes later they were sitting in his living room, both with a beer in their hands. The mood had definitely simmered since their moments in his truck.

"I like this house. It's not what I expected though."

He took a swig of beer, leaning back against the couch. "In what way?"

"I don't know. It's not as…*bachelor* as I

would have expected."

He was quiet for a moment. "About that."

"About what?" she asked, leaning forward. Then her eyes grew wide. "You're not going to tell me you're married, are you?"

He almost choked on his beer. "No!"

She looked relieved. "Thank God."

"I was engaged though." He avoided her gaze.

"Okay," she responded.

"And we bought a house together before we broke up." He spit the words out quickly.

She didn't say anything, so he glanced at her out of the corner of his eye. She was clearly waiting for him to say more.

He let out a sigh. "We bought *this* house. And then we broke up."

"I'm not sure what you're trying to tell me here." She dangled her beer bottle in between her fingers.

He shrugged his shoulders. "It's not a big deal. Not really. But she lives here. In the spare room." He waited for her to explode.

When she didn't react at all, he lifted his head. She was staring at him as though he were out of his mind.

"I could have lied to you. I'm not good with lies. We've been broken up since Kaylee cheated on me with a doctor that works at Seattle General. She's a nurse there. That was a year ago."

"Wow," was all she said.

He figured he may as well go for broke. "I want her out. I've tried for a year to get her out. She refuses to let me buy her interest. And I refuse to let her buy mine."

"So, you're telling me that you live with your ex-fiancé."

Things sounded much worse coming out of her mouth. "Not *living with*, really. We share a house."

He wasn't sure what he expected her to do now. Run for the door, maybe. But she didn't. She just leaned back against the couch and sipped her beer quietly. "Are you going to go psycho on me when I least expect it?" His brow arched.

"I hardly know you," she said.

The words bothered him. "I'm trying to change that."

"I realize that." She gave him half a smile. "You didn't have to tell me about her. Like you said, you could have lied."

"I told you, I'm not good with lying." He set his beer bottle down and leaned back next to her. "So, what are you thinking?"

"I'm trying not to think." She let her gaze roam over his face. It stopped on his lips.

Immediately he felt that intense pull of attraction again. He smiled halfway. "You're beautiful."

"It's nice that you think so."

He leaned toward her, their mouths touching gently. As the kiss deepened, he felt her relax. She let him take her beer bottle and set it on the coffee table.

He lifted a hand and tangled it in her hair, pulling her closer so that she climbed into his lap. As soon as she was settled against him, he felt a little of his control evaporate.

The kissing went on for a while. He kept his hands in respectable places until she lifted her mouth from his. She breathed deeply, grinding her hips in a delicious motion that had him sliding a hand up her abdomen toward a breast. When his fingers cupped her gently, she moaned, her mouth sliding against his again. "We should stop."

But she didn't stop. She drifted her own hands up his rib cage, taking his t-shirt with it. He didn't think twice, he pulled the shirt over his head, tossing it onto the floor beside the couch.

Things moved quickly after that. Her shirt was discarded next. He lowered one bra cup, his mouth latching onto her breast. The minute he slid his tongue over her sensitive skin, she threw her head back and let out a groan. He did the same thing to the other breast, his fingers making quick work of removing her bra.

He started to lower her back on the couch, prepared to slide over on top of her. She stopped him.

"What if your..." Her voice broke off. "What if somebody comes home?"

His sex muddled brain comprehended the words and he realized she was right. He moved off the couch, grabbing her by the hand. Then he tugged her down the hallway to the master bedroom. Once they were inside, he flipped the lock on the door, and gently pushed her up against it. Their mouths melted together quickly. He lifted her, grinding his hips against hers roughly enough to get a moan out of her. She reached for his belt, yanked at the buckle.

"Are you sure you don't want to just talk?" he asked against her mouth, his tongue dipping between her teeth as he said the words.

"No talking. It's overrated." She dragged his buckle open. A second later, her hand cupped him through the denim and he mumbled an oath. He turned, finding the bed and depositing her on it quickly. Then he went for the snap to her jeans. Before long, they were on the floor, along with her panties.

He looked her over for few moments, just enjoying the sight of her body. Then he flicked the buttons to his jeans open one by one, before dragging them down, his eyes never leaving hers. When he lowered himself onto the bed, she reached for him. He met her halfway in a deep and thorough kiss that had them both gasping for air.

He reached for his nightstand. After he'd sheathed himself, he grasped her hips and lifted them slightly. Poised at her entrance, he gently pushed inside her. He didn't stop until he was buried to the hilt.

She let out a small groan, grasping his shoulders as he started to move. The tension between them began to build. With each thrust, the pleasure grew stronger. He slid a hand over her collar bone, down across her breast, letting his lips trail along behind him. The moment his mouth latched onto her, he felt her come apart, her legs wrapping around him tightly. That was all that was needed to push him over the edge. He stilled, dropping his head to her chest as he exploded with a groan.

For several seconds, they lay there, still connected, breathing hard. He didn't want to move, but he knew he was heavy. He lifted up, carefully disengaging himself. When their eyes met, he saw the look of content satisfaction in hers. It was the most erotic thing he'd ever seen. "You're right, talking is overrated."

She chuckled at that.

He slid off her and onto his back. Then he waited for her to come undone with a slew of regrets.

Surprisingly, she didn't. She curled against his side, her hand resting against his chest. "Are you going to be insulted if I take a little nap?"

He tucked her head neatly underneath his chin. "Not at all. Have at it."

A moment later, he knew she had finally hit a wall. She was fast asleep.

13

Casey woke up to the sound of voices. He knew immediately that he and Aria weren't alone anymore. When he glanced at the bedside clock, he saw that it was almost four in the afternoon. They'd been asleep for a few hours.

He glanced down to where Aria was still sleeping soundly, her head resting in the crook of his arm. He hated to wake her. He knew she hadn't had much sleep over the past couple of weeks. He also knew she'd probably want to get back to the hospital soon.

The voices in the living room grew louder. Kaylee was definitely home. He was going to have to get rid of her before Aria woke up. He didn't want to worry about any confrontations. He knew how Kaylee could be.

He slid Aria's head gently onto the pillow and climbed out of bed. After he'd thrown on a pair of jeans, he searched for his t-shirt. That was when he realized they'd left a trail of their clothes in the living room.

"Shit," he muttered, knowing things were going to be even more complicated now.

He glanced at Aria one last time and then opened his door and stepped out into the hallway, carefully closing it behind him. He barely had the time to take a breath before Kaylee was on him, her eyes full of fury.

"You bastard!" Her hand connected with his face so suddenly that he didn't even see it coming. When she reached up to swing at him again, he caught her wrist in his hand. Now he was pissed.

"What the fuck?"

"You've got somebody in there, don't you?"

He gave her a gentle shove in the other direction, but she came back at him.

"You need to back off." He sidestepped her and entered the living room. He was surprised to find nobody there. He could have sworn he'd heard Kaylee arguing with someone.

"I can't believe you would bring a woman here," she snapped, coming up behind him.

He turned in time to block another blow.

This time she was aiming for his head. He grabbed her wrists roughly, using as much restraint as he could manage to keep from really hurting her. "Don't hit me again." His eyes bored into hers. He couldn't remember ever being this angry.

She seemed to realize she'd pushed too far. Suddenly she burst into tears. "I'm sorry. I didn't mean to. I love you. I always have."

He didn't feel even the slightest sliver of pity for her. "Have you completely lost your mind?" He let her go and she dissolved into a puddle of tears in a corner of the couch.

At a loss, he stared at her for a moment, finally realizing just how seriously screwed up she was. He'd made a big mistake by staying here in the house for the past year. He'd only made things worse.

Leaning over, he grabbed the clothes he and Aria had discarded earlier.

"Who is she?" Kaylee asked, sniffling as she watched him.

"Never mind who she is." He straightened. "While it's beside the point, I know you're seeing all kinds of guys, Kaylee. You're not sitting around pining over me. We've been over for a long time. You're going to have to accept that."

"I can't."

"You don't have a choice." He shook his

head, doing his best to keep his voice down. He absolutely didn't want Aria hearing any of this. "I'm not in love with you. You're not in love with me, either."

"That's not true," she sobbed. "I am. I can't handle being without you."

"You're going to have to, Kaylee. I don't know what I've been thinking, playing these games with you for the last year. My brothers tried to tell me. So did my sister. I didn't listen. I wanted this fucking house so badly that I thought I could wait you out." He shook his head in disgust. "But I can't. I'm done. You can have it. I'm moving out." He turned and headed for the bedroom, knowing he was going to have to wake Aria up and get her out of here somehow. Kaylee wasn't going to make that easy.

"No!" Kaylee flew after him, her nails catching him in the back as he reached his doorway. He rounded on her, trying to keep his temper in check. She nailed him with a decent amount of force and he hit his door, just as it began to open. He fell into his bedroom, hitting the floor with a thud, Kaylee landing on top of him.

Aria stood in the doorway, her face a mask of confusion. She wore nothing but one of his old t-shirts. He realized why quickly. He had most of her clothing in his hand.

"You bitch!" Kaylee scrambled to her feet and headed straight for Aria, who just stood there, completely stricken.

Casey reacted quickly, having no intention of letting Kaylee take a swipe at Aria next. He snagged her around the middle and yanked her back. "Enough!"

"I hate you!" she screamed at him, completely coming undone. "I hate you! I hate you! I hate you!"

Casey shoved Kaylee in the other direction and tossed a glance at Aria, his eyes filled with regret. "Get dressed." He spoke quietly, knowing he was too embarrassed and angry to say anything more at that point.

She sidestepped him and grabbed her clothing from the floor where he'd dropped it a few moments earlier. Then she disappeared into the bathroom.

He turned to Kaylee, an anger he didn't even realize he could feel, boiling over. "You need to leave. *Now*. While you're gone, I'll get my shit. Don't try to find me. Don't try to talk to me. You and me? We're done. Do you understand?"

She started to shake her head.

"Do you fucking understand me?" He glared down at her.

Her eyes turned cold and she wiped at the mascara that was running down her face. "Yes, you asshole. I understand you!"

"Good."

He turned away from her just as Aria stepped out of the bathroom, now fully dressed. To say she looked uncomfortable was the understatement of the century.

He let out a sigh and motioned for her to follow him. Before they reached the front door someone was pounding on it. The police, he realized, as he glanced out the front window.

The freaking police were on his front porch.

. . .

Aria cradled a cup of coffee between her fingers. She was curled up in a chair in a corner of the kids' hospital room. Unfortunately she wasn't alone with them. Her mother was seated in the chair between the two beds, her knitting yarn in her hands again. Aria wasn't sure what the deal was with that. To her knowledge, her mother had never knitted before in her life.

She reminded herself that she hadn't seen the woman in thirteen years. Perhaps she did knit now.

Regardless, the pair hadn't spoken since Aria had arrived at the hospital a few hours earlier. Aria had considered sitting in the waiting room again. She really wasn't in the mood to deal with Adele. In the end, she'd decided she was here to spend time with the kids so that's what she was going to do — whether her mother liked it or not.

Only the kids were asleep. They'd both nodded off right after she'd arrived.

"You don't have to sit here and breathe down my neck," Adele said, breaking the silence. "What is it that you think is going to happen here while you're gone?"

"I don't think anything is going to happen while I'm gone," Aria said quietly. "I'm here for the kids. It has nothing to do with you."

Adele obviously didn't believe that. She rolled her eyes.

"I'm not going to placate you right now. I have bigger problems."

"Of course you do. Always thinking of yourself. Some things never change."

Aria's temper flared. "*I* always think of *myself*?"

"What's that supposed to mean?"

Aria counted to ten inside of her head. "Never mind," she snapped, knowing it wasn't a good idea for them to get into an argument in the room with the kids.

"No, please enlighten me. I realize you hold a grudge against me. So I wasn't perfect as a parent. Your father wasn't perfect, either."

"I have no beef with him anymore. He's

dead."

"So when I die, you'll forgive me?"

Hearing the words out loud made Aria realize how ridiculous the idea sounded. "I don't need to forgive you, Mother. Not if you actually acknowledged there was a problem. But you don't."

"How could I acknowledge anything with you? You left."

"I left because I couldn't take things anymore. The drinking, the violence."

Adele opened her mouth, then shut it again. She turned back to her yarn silently.

"It's been years, just forget it," Aria said sulkily.

"Will *you* forget about it?"

No, Aria thought to herself.

"I want custody of the children, Aria."

The words cut into Aria like a knife. She narrowed her eyes. She glanced over at Tiffany. The child appeared to be asleep. But was she listening to this entire conversation? "I'm not going to talk about this here."

"I've already told the kids. They want to live with me."

Anger coursed through Aria. "Lyla did not leave the children to you."

"She wasn't thinking straight. The children know me. We have a relationship. I can provide for them. What do you have to offer them?"

Aria had asked herself that very question only days ago. She hadn't come up with too many answers. But last night, at dinner with Casey—thanks to him—she'd realized that it wasn't really about what *she* thought she could offer the kids, it was about what *Lyla* had thought she could offer the kids.

"I'm their grandmother. I love them. I should have a say in what happens here," Adele said matter-of-factly.

"Lyla's will is a legal document, Mother. You can contest it if you want. But you're going against what *she* wanted."

"So now you suddenly want the children? Why? Because I'm here?"

"That has nothing to do with it."

"Well according to the social worker, you were considering send them into foster care not two days ago. According to *her*, you told her you simply couldn't take the children home."

Aria straightened, now getting angry. "She shouldn't have told you any of that. My conversations with her are private."

"She's looking out for the kids. That's her job."

Frustrated, Aria stood up. "If Lyla had wanted you to have the kids, she would have said so in her will."

"Like I said, she wasn't thinking straight."

"So if I say I'll take the kids, you're going to fight me for them?" Aria's eyes grew wide as she watched her mother's lips pinch together. She didn't say a word. But Aria could read her like a book.

So angry she could barely see straight, Aria spun on her heel and left the room before she said something worse that she really ended up regretting.

Stepping into the hallway, she saw a woman standing at the front nurses station. There was something familiar about her, though Aria couldn't put her finger on what. When the woman saw her, she walked in her direction. She stopped in front of Aria when they met in the middle of the hallway.

"Aria, right?"

Aria gave her a questioning look.

"I'm Colby Gage."

Aria immediately realized this was Casey's sister. The resemblance was uncanny.

"You okay?"

She wasn't. Not really. Her day was turning out to be far more than she was prepared for. "I'm fine. How can I help you?"

Colby was quiet for a moment. "Do you have time for a cup of coffee? I was hoping we could talk."

Aria wasn't sure that was such a good idea. After the debacle that had occurred at Casey's house earlier, she wasn't sure how involved she wanted to be in his situation. As much as she liked him, she had enough problems of her own.

"I know you're probably upset about what happened earlier. I would be, too."

Aria had done her best to forget about what had happened that afternoon. She didn't want to think about the fact that Casey's ex had gone nuts, attacking both of them. She didn't want to think about the fact that a concerned neighbor had called 911 and the police had shown up and cuffed Casey, either—or about the fact that they'd hauled him off in a squad car. "I'm not upset. Not about him anyway."

Colby indicated that Aria follow her down the hallway.

Reluctantly, she did.

There was a cafeteria two floors down. When they were seated at a small table in a corner of the large room, two coffees in front of them, Colby let out a sigh. "He's not in jail. He's got friends in the right places and they figured the whole mess out."

Aria figured she was probably talking about Nick Holt. She didn't question that. She just nodded. "That's good."

"Thank God you were there. Your statements to the responding officers helped."

"If I hadn't been there, there's a good chance

she wouldn't have gone crazy in the first place."

"Kaylee is crazy anyway," Colby said firmly. "She's been an anchor on Casey's foot for the past year now."

"He explained the situation," Aria said, staring down into the cup of coffee she held. She really wasn't sure she needed any more caffeine. She'd already had more than her share for the day.

"I'm sure he explained the *Casey* version things." Colby straightened, her expression serious. "My brother is a good guy, Aria. The best. He's kind and caring and honest. For about five minutes, he and Kaylee were good for each other. Then she cheated. He broke things off, but she's refused to quit claim the house. And so has he. He thought he could wait things out until she found some schmuck and left. I think he finally realized today that's not going to happen. It was a harsh slap of reality for him."

Aria had seen that for herself. "I appreciate you taking the time to explain all this to me, but he really did tell me himself. The bottom line is that I don't know him very well."

"But you're into him."

Aria found herself frowning. She wasn't sure how to respond.

"I know I'm being nosy. Casey would kill me if he knew I was here. But I love him and I want to see him happy. For the past couple of days, he's been different." Colby shrugged her shoulders. "In other words, he's had a good time with you. He brought you home to his house."

"So? I'm sure he's brought a lot of women to his house before."

"No. Just you. For a year he's played it safe. Obviously he likes you enough to say the hell with things."

Aria was a little surprised by the words. Especially since Casey had been so open with her about his ex. She hedged a little, then shrugged her shoulders. "I don't know him very well," she repeated. "And he doesn't know me well, either."

"But you slept together."

Aria felt her skin grow hot.

"I know I'm out of line talking to you like this, but I know how my brother is. He's going to take a step back now. He's embarrassed and angry — not at you — at himself. I don't want to see him wreck a good thing before it's even gotten the chance to get started."

"I'm practically a stranger to him — to you," Aria argued.

"Yes, well, most of the people we risk our lives for every day are strangers. And then they're not."

The words made sense in a crazy kind of

way. "My life is a mess right now," Aria finally said honestly. "I'm in the middle of a very touchy situation. My mother is here now and making things worse. I've got a fulltime job that I need to concentrate on. I really don't have room for any more commotion in my world."

Colby nodded. "I hear you. I just hope you'll think about things. Clearly you have feelings for Casey. You don't seem like the type of girl that would go home with him if you didn't."

Aria didn't confirm or deny that.

"Just so you know, he moved out of his house today." Colby stood, giving Aria a sympathetic look. "He's staying with my brother, Trent, for the time being." She was gone a moment later.

Aria sat there in silence for a few moments. The truth was, as much as she tried to tell herself that getting any further involved with Casey would be a mistake, she still found herself attracted to him. That fact was maddening, and she let out a sigh. She tossed her coffee cup into the trash and headed for the exit. She had more pressing things to deal with. For one, speaking with her sister's attorney. If her mother planned to fight her for the kids, then she supposed she was going to have to fight back.

14

Casey stared at the television blankly. He was sitting on the couch in his brother's house, a beer in his hand that he had barely touched. He wasn't in the mood for a beer and he wasn't in the mood for the football game that was broadcasting across the screen. In fact, he wasn't in the mood for any company, either. But this was Trent's house. There wasn't much he could do about his brother's presence.

"What's done is done. You may as well quit sulking about it."

"That's some real wisdom. Thanks."

Trent gave him a look. "Dude, I warned you about all this. For the past year, I've told you to walk away—that no house is worth what you've been through. Just what in the hell did you think was going to happen?"

"She cheated. I thought she'd eventually take off with the bastard and leave me the hell alone."

Trent made a noise of disbelief. "You did not. You're not stupid, Casey. You saw what we all saw. You just didn't want to admit it."

"I didn't see *this* coming. I never would have taken Aria into the house today if I'd thought Kaylee was capable of what happened."

"I'll give you that. I didn't see her losing her mind that way, either. But it doesn't surprise me. She thinks she's in love with you. She got desperate when you finally moved on and didn't try to hide it."

"Tell me something I don't know."

"At least Nick got you off the hook."

Casey immediately took offense to the words. "I was never on the hook! I didn't lay a hand on Kaylee except in self-defense. She slapped me, punched me, scratched me—and then she went after Aria. What was I supposed to do, let her beat the shit out of us?"

"No," Trent said firmly. "I didn't say you did anything wrong. The cops know that, too. But you should have pressed charges against her for domestic abuse. She's not going to go away."

Casey had thought about pressing charges against Kaylee. He'd been mad enough to at the time. But he'd walked away instead. He'd gotten a lot of his things from the house. The rest of his stuff he would have to worry about later. For now, he just wanted his ex to disappear. And she'd promised the police she was going to—at least as far as Casey was concerned.

"What about the other chick?"

Casey's brow furrowed. He'd been thinking about Aria all day long. He knew he owed her one hell of an apology. The thing was, he had no idea how to go about that. What had happened in front of her was so awful, he didn't even know where to start. So he was avoiding the confrontation all together. Besides, most likely she had run for the hills. That's what he would have done if their roles were reversed.

"You're into her. She's into you. What's the deal?" Trent prodded.

"If you're talking about Aria, I think you can safely eliminate her from my equation."

"It wasn't your fault what happened."

"If you were her, would you want to see me again?" The words were a kick in the reality butt and Casey felt his depression deepen. He'd really liked Aria. But she had enough problems of her own and he wasn't about to drag her down further with his.

"She's got a lot of baggage herself. Maybe

you're better off this way."

Casey just scowled in response. In no mood for any more talking, he got up and left the room.

Trent had a spare bedroom that Casey had frequented over the past year. His stuff was now littered around it. He slammed the door behind him and sat down on the bed, raking a hand through his hair in frustration. How had the good day that had started out, turned into such a nightmare?

He couldn't wrap his head around an answer. Instead of thinking about it further, he leaned back on bed and shut his eyes, willing sleep to take over and clear his head of all rational thought.

. . .

Aria placed a call to Daniel Ronson, who this time, didn't answer the phone. It was Sunday and he'd told her the day before he didn't normally work weekends. She waited for voicemail and left a message. "Mr. Ronson, it's Aria Carlisle. I need to speak with you as soon as possible. I've made a decision regarding the children. There are some new developments we need to discuss." She rattled off her number, then hung up.

She knew she needed to figure things out quickly. Now that Jaden was awake, both kids were likely going to be released from the hospital soon—in a few days, if Joanne Sutcliffe was right. Adele or no Adele, arrangements had to be made.

She set her phone down on the kitchen table. She was home now. She'd spent most of the afternoon at the hospital, in spite of the fact that she didn't have any desire to be near her mother. Adele was acting as though their earlier conversation hadn't happened. She didn't mention getting custody of the children again. But the notion hung in the air between them like a bad smell.

Aria ran a hand through her hair and sighed in frustration. She was beside herself at this point. A little over two weeks ago, she'd had all her ducks in a row. Her job was going great, her finances were good. She'd been so happy and content. Now, she felt anxious and lost. Everywhere she turned, was another obstacle.

Her thoughts roamed to Casey for the hundredth time that day. She didn't want to think about him. She'd ordered herself not to…and failed.

When she'd followed him to his house that afternoon, she'd known what was going to happen. She'd wanted to sleep with him. The attraction between them was hot and heavy and impossible to ignore. Even now, she felt a shimmer or awareness as she remembered the way his lips had felt against hers, the way his hands had felt roaming over her skin—the way he'd felt pumping inside her.

Her skin heated and she chastised herself. It was sex, plain and simple. He obviously felt the same way because he hadn't gotten a hold of her.

She supposed she'd never given him her cell phone number. She hadn't gotten the chance. She knew Detective Holt had it. If Casey wanted it, she doubted he'd have much trouble worming it out of his friend.

But so far, he hadn't.

She thought about what Colby Gage had said to her earlier about Casey taking a step back. She guessed she couldn't blame him there. He was embarrassed. She understood that, too. She was embarrassed for him.

Hearing her phone ring, she glanced at it. The number calling was unknown and immediately she had flashbacks of the night before. "Hello?"

"Ms. Carlisle? This is Brad Armbrust. We met yesterday when you came to the office to meet with Daniel Ronson, my associate."

Aria remembered the man instantly—and the unsettled vibe she'd gotten off of him. She found herself frowning. "Mr. Armbrust. Is there something I can do for you?"

"Actually, I'm returning your call. Daniel is

unavailable. I'm handling his business for the day."

Aria wasn't thrilled about the prospect of dealing with Brad Armbrust. She hadn't liked the man when she'd met him. "I'd rather deal with Mr. Ronson. We had a lengthy discussion about things yesterday and I'd rather not have to re-hash the situation with someone else."

"There won't be a need for that. Daniel has briefed me. I thought perhaps you and I should meet. It's my understanding that the children will be released soon. Is that correct?"

"Possibly in the next few days," she said reluctantly. She really didn't want to deal with a different attorney, but she supposed under the circumstances she had no choice. Not with Adele breathing down her neck. "Listen, I have some complications here. I mentioned that in my message. While I've decided that I will take responsibility for the children, my mother is in town. She has decided to fight me on that."

"You mean she's going to contest the will," he clarified.

"I suppose that's the legal term for things, yes. Does she have a leg to stand on?"

Armbrust was quiet for a moment. "Possibly. But the law is in your favor, provided your sister's will is in order. I really think we should meet as soon as possible and iron out things. How about if I come to you this time?"

"That's not necessary. I don't mind meeting you someplace."

"Nonsense. I'm on my way out anyway." He paused, and she heard the rustle of papers in the background. "I don't see your address here."

"I'm not sure I gave it to Mr. Ronson." She was a little hesitant. She didn't really know this guy and he'd given her an odd feeling when she'd met him the day before. But he was an attorney and he was right; they needed to iron things out for the kids sooner rather than later. She rambled her address off quickly.

"Give me thirty minutes."

Aria hung up, feeling tense and uncertain about what she was doing. She'd meant what she'd told Casey the day before about making the situation with the children work once she brought them home. There was no turning back. There was a small part of her that wondered if Adele wasn't a better option for them.

She quickly reminded herself of her own childhood. Maybe Adele had changed. Maybe she wasn't a drunk anymore and maybe she wasn't violent. But Lyla hadn't left custody to her and Aria figured there had to be a reason for that.

The sound of the front doorbell jarred her

out of her thoughts. She checked her watch. She'd only gotten off the phone with Brad Armbrust a few minutes earlier. He couldn't possibly have made it across town that quickly, even on a Sunday.

Aria walked into the living room. She glanced through the window in the top of her door. She didn't see anyone there. Frowning, she opened the door and peeked outside. Before she could so much as blink, Kaylee Simmons stepped out from behind a large hydrangea.

"I'm here to apologize," she said quickly, when Aria started to back away from her.

"You don't owe me anything," was Aria's response. She grasped the handle of her front door, prepared to step inside and slam it shut.

"I know you don't want to talk to me and that I freaked you out earlier. I promise I'm not here for any trouble."

"How do you know where I live?" Aria asked, ignoring the woman's rambling.

Kaylee fidgeted a little. "Casey and I live together. We share everything."

Aria felt a sick feeling in her stomach. She was sensing this woman's desperation. She didn't appear sorry for her behavior earlier at all. "You should go."

"I didn't mean for what happened earlier to happen." Kaylee reached up and tucked her short blonde hair behind her ear. "I just lost it when I saw him with you. You can understand that. I mean he and I were engaged once. We've been living together. I've had a hard time letting go."

Aria backed up a little more. "Your issues with Casey have nothing to do with me."

"They do," Kaylee said emphatically. "You're distracting him."

This woman was truly certifiable. "You need to leave or I'm going to call the police."

"I already told you, I'm not here to cause trouble. I'm just letting you know where I stand on things. Casey's gone for now. But he'll be back. He loves that house. He loves me. He just doesn't realize it yet."

"That's great," Aria said, stepping into her house. She started to shut the door but Kaylee leaned forward and inserted her foot, keeping Aria from shutting her out.

"Don't get in my way."

The words chilled Aria to the bone and she finally lost her patience. "Get your foot out of my door or I'm calling the police."

Kaylee snickered, keeping her foot firmly in place.

"Is there a problem here?"

Aria was so rattled that she hadn't noticed Brad Armbrust drive up. He was standing behind Kaylee now, an interested but concerned look on his face.

Kaylee whirled around, startled. She shot a glare his way. "There's no problem. I was just leaving."

Armbrust stepped aside so Kaylee could pass. She sauntered down the sidewalk and climbed into a green Prius. A moment later she sped off down the street.

"Did I interrupt something?" Armbrust asked, stepping up onto the porch.

"Yes, thank you." Aria opened the door wider, a lot happier to see him today than she had been yesterday.

He stepped into her foyer, a black briefcase in his hand. "Trouble comes in all shapes and sizes, I guess."

Aria knew what he meant by the words. Kaylee was attractive as hell. Blonde and tall and stacked. She was everything Aria wasn't.

Shoving that fact aside, Aria considered him. "I'm not sure what we need to do here. My mother is threatening me. I don't have a lot of money to fight this type of thing in court, Mr. Armbrust."

He gestured to her kitchen table. "Let's you and I go over a few things."

She followed him to the table and took a seat across from him. He dug through his briefcase for a moment, then pulled out a stack of papers. "So, the wills are in order. I looked over everything before I headed your way. Your sister and her husband were very explicit about their wishes. That's good news. Your mother will be the one having to deal with court costs and attorney fees. You really have nothing to fight."

Aria felt a huge sense of relief.

"That being said," he continued, "Daniel expressed your reluctance as far as the kids are concerned. What made you change your mind?"

Aria wasn't sure she owed him an explanation. Still, he had come all the way across town. She shrugged. "I've thought things over. It's what my sister wanted. I just needed to get my head together and be sure I was doing the right thing."

He waited for her to say more.

"It was a big decision, Mr. Armbrust. I wanted to make sure I was the best person to take the children. Now I feel certain that I am."

"I knew your sister's husband. Very well, in fact. We handled a lot of cases together. Kevin was a good man."

"So I've heard. I never knew him."

"He was a risk taker. That's what made him such a good attorney." He leaned back in his chair. "How are the children by the way? I've been meaning to stop in and see them — bring them a trinket or two on behalf of the firm.

Maybe I still will."

"They're doing better. They'll probably be released in a few days."

"Well, that's wonderful. Things seemed pretty dismal there for a while."

She didn't bother arguing with him. "So what happens if my mother files a suit?"

He snapped his briefcase shut, leaving a copy of the will lying on her table. "It's very difficult to contest a will, Ms. Carlisle. Dead people can't speak. Unless your mother is able to convince a judge that your sister and her husband weren't in their right minds at the time these wills were drawn up, she doesn't stand a chance. And I can assure you, Kevin and Lyla were very much in their right minds. I helped them draw the wills up myself." He gave her an honest smile. "I'm going to leave this copy here for you. Refer to it if you need to. In the meantime, I wouldn't worry too much. These types of situations always bring out the worst in people."

"When my mother threatens something, she typically follows through."

"If she does, we'll have your back." He stood. "I'm glad you called. I appreciate you taking the time to meet with me."

"It is Sunday. I should be thanking you."

"Not necessary. I'll be in touch."

She walked him to the door, still a little

uneasy. She could only hope Kaylee wasn't lurking somewhere outside, waiting to pounce once Armbrust was gone.

She shut and locked the door the moment he hit the porch. Then she watched through the window carefully as he climbed into his upper-end Mercedes and a seconds later, sped off down the street.

The silence in the house was deafening. It immediately put her nerves on edge. She considered going back to the hospital, just to be around people. In the end, she decided against that idea. She needed to get some sleep, in her own bed. Another thing Casey had been right about was the fact that she was close to bottoming out.

She made a point of checking the rest of the windows and doors. Everything was secure. After shutting down the lights, she headed into her bathroom and drew herself a hot bath. She added a splash of scented bubbles and undressed. Then she slid down into the hot water and leaned her head back, relishing in the feel of the soothing liquid against her tense muscles. She immediately began to relax. It didn't take long for her to doze off.

Minutes went by, or maybe an hour, she wasn't sure. What she did know is that a noise jarred her awake. When she glanced at the phone next to the tub, she realized she'd been in the bath for almost an hour. The water was getting tepid.

She sat up straight, sloshing water up over the edge of the clawfoot, and stared around the bathroom. Nothing was out of place. All was quiet.

Had she dreamed the noise?

Her skin was suddenly chilled and she reached over and pulled the plug on the bath tub. She climbed over the side and reached for her bathrobe. Once she was snuggled inside the terry cloth, she felt a little bit better. The noise had probably been outside—or maybe she'd imagined it all together. After the past few days and what she'd been through, it wouldn't be a shocker if she were imagining things.

She went into her bedroom and pulled on a fresh pair of pajamas. Then she went to the kitchen for a glass of water.

She noticed right away something was wrong. The minute she stepped into the living room, the hairs on the back of her neck stood on end.

She started to turn around, to head back to the bedroom for her phone. She didn't get the chance. Someone grabbed her from behind.

She instantly tried to scream, but a hand came over her mouth hard. She instinctively bit down. Her teeth encountered thick, black leather. She made an indent, and the hand lowered abruptly. She started to scream instantly. This time the hand didn't bother covering her mouth. Instead, it slammed hard against her face, propelling her back against the art deco fireplace in the corner.

Stunned, Aria felt herself falling. Her head hit a corner of the hearth and then everything went black.

15

Casey heard the banging on the bedroom door. He groaned, grabbing a pillow and slapping it tightly over his head. He didn't want to talk to anyone else. Trent had said his piece. Colby had been by earlier. Brandon had phoned. All he was missing was two bits from his parents. He wasn't sure he could take that at this point.

"Open the fucking door. It's me."

He recognized Nick's voice and scowled. "If you're coming to take me to jail, it's too late. You had your chance."

"Aria was attacked, Casey. At her house. It's not good."

The words scared the shit out of Casey and he was on his feet in seconds. He flipped the lock and whipped the door open. "What did you say?"

"I said, Aria was attacked at her house. B&E. She's banged up. Call came in an hour ago."

Casey felt panicked. "Is she okay?"

"Like I said, she's banged up. A couple officers are on the scene already. I'm heading over there. I thought you might want to go with me."

Casey hesitated. "I'm not sure she'll want to see me. After what happened today—"

"She's upset and scared. Obviously there's something going on between you two whether you want to admit it or not. I could use a little help here."

"Okay," Casey agreed without giving it much thought. He did care about Aria. Yes, their relationship had gotten off to a rocky start, but Nick was right, they had a connection.

The ride to her house was brisk. When they both drove up, it seemed like all the lights in the place were on. There were multiple police cars out front. The scene was scary as hell from Casey's point of view.

"Just be supportive," Nick instructed as they headed up the walk. "That's what you're here for."

Casey remained silent as he followed Nick to the porch and through the front door.

The house was packed with police. Casey counted five officers right off the bat. One female officer sat on the couch. Aria sat next to her, wrapped in a blanket. When Casey got a look at her face, he immediately saw red. It was bruised and battered. She looked like she'd been through an episode of *Ultimate Fighter*. He froze for a moment, not sure what to say or do.

"Give me a minute with her," Nick instructed, glancing from officer to officer.

Apparently he was in charge because they cleared the room quickly.

Aria lifted her head, her eyes immediately locking with Casey's.

At that moment, it hit him hard. She wasn't just a fling for him—a one-night-stand. He had some serious feelings for her. And he had absolutely no idea what to do about them.

Nick walked over and took a seat in the chair next to her. "I have to ask you some questions. Do you need anything first?"

She looked away from Casey and met Nick's gaze. "No."

"Okay. Tell me what happened."

She pulled the blanket tighter around herself, looking at Casey again. "What are you doing here?"

"I asked him to come," Nick said before Casey could reply. "Do you want him to go?"

She was hesitant. Casey saw that right away. She was on the fence about him now. That fact bothered him a lot more than he wanted it to.

"I saw Kaylee earlier." The words came out softly but she may as well have screamed them.

Casey felt anger course through him in waves.

Nick stood, turning and giving Casey a look. "You need to go outside."

"You asked me to come here," Casey said quietly. His eyes were still locked on Aria's.

"Maybe I made a mistake."

"Are you saying Kaylee did this to you?" Casey ignored Nick.

"No. I don't know." She shook her head, clearly confused. She was still in shock, Casey realized. He'd seen enough people in her state during his years with the fire department. He knew what shock looked like. Forcing himself to remain calm, he walked over and crouched down in front of her. "What happened?"

"I was in the bathtub. I fell asleep." Her hands started to shake and she clasped them tightly in front of her. "I heard a noise. I thought it was outside. When I went into the living room, somebody grabbed me from behind." She leaned over, resting her head between her knees, and breathed deeply.

When Casey got a look at the back of her head, he grimaced. There was a good-sized knot there. "Did she get this checked out?" he asked, tossing a look over his shoulder at Nick.

"I doubt it. She's been here the entire time.

Nobody called an ambulance. She refused it."

Casey moved so that he sat next to her on the couch. "You've got a pretty good knot on the back of your head."

"I fell down. Someone hit me and I smacked my head on the hearth." She forced herself back into a sitting position.

"Who? Aria? Who hit you? Was it Kaylee?"

"I don't know. Whoever it was, they were a lot bigger than me."

Casey thought that over. Kaylee was a lot bigger than Aria. "What did you mean about Kaylee?"

"She was here. Earlier. She was upset about what happened at your house." She sniffled a little. "She says she loves you. She's been following you — I don't know for how long. That's how she knows where I live."

Casey felt a wave of nausea wash over him. He felt second wave of anger and forced himself to tamp it down.

"You're going to have to be more specific," Nick said, sitting down again. "Start at the beginning and go from there. What happened when you got home tonight? And what time was it?"

Aria took a deep breath. "It was after five. I argued with my mother. I wanted to stay at the hospital but we had words. She wants the kids." She looked over at Casey. "She said she's going to sue me for custody."

This was interesting news. Casey frowned at that. "Why would she do that? Your sister appointed you as their guardian."

"She says Lyla wasn't in her right mind."

"So you got mad and left," Nick encouraged, clearly growing impatient.

"I didn't want to deal with her anymore. We were fighting in front of the kids…" Her voice trailed off. "I came home—called Lyla's attorney. He wasn't in. His associate called me back instead. Brad Armbrust." She was quiet for a moment. "When I told him what my mother was up to, he told me he was familiar with my case. He wanted to meet me and discuss things—here at my house." She kept her face averted from Casey's. "Kaylee showed up before he got here. I thought she was him."

Casey felt instant fury. He stood up, unable to sit still anymore. Nick shot him a warning look but he ignored it. There was no question about it, he was going to strangle Kaylee.

"Did she attack you?" Nick asked carefully.

"She apologized," Aria shocked both men by saying.

"Apologized," Nick repeated. "Sincerely?"

"At first. Then she got upset when I didn't respond the way she wanted." She paused, then looked at Casey again. "She told me she's in love with you—that you love her, too. She started to get pretty upset. At that point the attorney showed up. She got spooked and took off."

Casey opened his mouth to speak but no words came out. He was so upset he couldn't even talk.

"You really should go outside," Nick said, starting to stand up again.

"She's a fucking lunatic," Casey exclaimed, muttering a string of curses. "I should have pressed charges—put her in jail. None of this would have happened if I had."

"Do you think Kaylee's the person who attacked you?" Nick asked, ignoring Casey.

"I told you, I don't know. The person was significantly bigger than me. But I'm not a large person."

"Kaylee's significantly bigger than she is," Casey pointed out angrily. "She's probably got fifty pounds on her."

"You're not sure if the person was a man or a woman?" Nick asked.

Casey could tell Aria wasn't. She shrugged her shoulders. "A lot of people are bigger than me. If I had to guess, I would think it was a man. But it happened so fast, I didn't see the person. Just felt them."

"Were the lights on or off?" Nick inquired.

"Off. I had the bedroom light on though. It provides decent light into the hallway and the living room. My back was to the person the whole time, except when I landed against the fireplace. All I caught a glimpse of then was a black mask."

Nick made a few notes, then stood up. "Did the person speak to you at any point during the attack?"

"No. But I heard breathing. Deep breathing, like the person was out of breath."

"So when you fell against the fireplace, the perp ran off?"

"I blacked out. I guess that's what happened. When I came to, I was alone. I called the police right away."

"Were your doors locked? Front and back?"

"Yes. I checked before I got in the tub. I was nervous because of Kaylee's visit. I remember doublechecking everything. Even the windows."

Nick thought that over. "What about a hide-a-key?"

Aria's skin instantly paled. "I have one."

"Where is it?"

"In the flower bed out front, under a potted plant." Her face fell. "I didn't even think about it being there. It's been there for years, since I moved in here."

"Okay. Give me a minute. I'll be right back." Nick disappeared through the front door.

Casey took a seat across from her. He shook his head in regret. "I'm sorry, Aria. This is all my fault."

"I can't say for sure that Kaylee attacked me, Casey. Whoever did was strong. I know I'm small but whoever grabbed me lifted me up off my feet without any trouble at all. Even though Kaylee's bigger than me, I'm not sure she could do that."

"She's got half a foot on you at least," Casey pointed out. He rubbed his hands over his face wearily. "I'm sorry," he said again, at a loss for words.

"Stop apologizing."

He let out a sigh. "You should put some ice on your face."

"It's not so bad."

He reached over and brushed some hair back from her face. "It's bad. It looks like it hurts like hell."

"Maybe a little." She leaned into his touch. He took that as a good sign.

"I was going to call you," he said after a long moment of silence. "I wasn't sure if you would speak to me after what happened this afternoon."

"It wasn't your fault."

"Yeah, actually it was. I should have let go of that house a long time ago. I was being stubborn and stupid." He dropped his hand back into his lap. "Kaylee's never gotten as crazy as she did today. She's never gotten violent. I think she realized things were really over and that pushed her over the edge." He looked at her again. "I never would have brought you to my house if I had thought she was going to come unglued that way."

"She's not going to let you go," she said quietly.

"She doesn't have a choice. I'm already gone." He stood abruptly. "You got any ice in your freezer?"

She nodded solemnly just as Nick came back into the room. Both Casey and Aria looked at him questioningly.

He held his fingers up. A silver key was clenched between them. "I wouldn't keep this out there anymore."

"You think that's how the person got in," she figured out.

"There's no sign of forced entry. Windows are all secure."

She took the key from him.

"You're not going to like this, but I have to ask. What about your mother?"

"You mean do I think she attacked me tonight?" she asked, her voice filled with disbelief.

Nick shrugged. "You said she's threatening you."

"She's threatening to sue me for custody of the kids. Trust me, she didn't attack me. I know that for sure."

"How?" Nick asked carefully.

She hesitated. "This may sound weird, but I can sense her. I always have been able to. She's got a very distinct scent to her. Gardenias. Besides, she's no bigger than I am."

"Okay," Nick relented. "We'll bring Kaylee in for questioning—also the attorney. If he was here earlier, I want to talk to him. Other than that, unless you have anything else for me…" His voice trailed off.

"The kids thought someone was in their room the other night. You don't think this is somehow connected, do you?"

Casey could tell Nick had considered the idea just by the frown on his face.

"I'm not sure. But the fact that you had an incident with your car right around that time, and now this…"

Casey didn't want to believe Kaylee was responsible for the attack on Aria. At the same time, he didn't want to believe a murdering maniac that had already killed two people and shot two children was on her tail, either.

"I'm not sure you should stay here alone tonight." Nick glanced down at his cell phone as it started to ring. Then he turned to Aria again. "You'd probably be better off staying with a friend."

"I'll figure something out. I won't stay here alone." She stood as Nick prepared to leave. "Thank you."

"No worries. Call me if you need me. You have my cell." He looked at Casey. "You good?"

"I've got my truck."

Nick left. The other officers followed suit.

Casey went into the kitchen and dug through her freezer until he found a bag of frozen peas. He brought them into the living room. Aria was back on the couch, her head in her hands.

He squatted down again, offering the bag to her.

She took it silently and gently pressed it against her face.

"I'm not leaving you here alone." He sat on the coffee table in front of her. "Come home with me."

"I'll go back to the hospital, Casey. I'll be fine."

"I mentioned to you that Kaylee is a nurse at Seattle General. I'd rather you stayed with me."

"That's not a good idea. I'll be safe enough. There's a cop guarding the kids."

"Why is it not a good idea for you to stay with me?" He knew why not. Still, he was ready to argue.

"You know why not."

"I have feelings for you. Those didn't just go away because of what happened today."

She lowered the bag from her face. "We both have really complicated lives right now. Basically, brewing storms. Do you think it's smart to combine two tornados?"

That was an interesting way of putting it. He found himself grinning halfway. "Probably not. But I seem to have developed a thing for you."

Her lips quirked. "You're nuts."

He reached forward, tipped her chin so she looked at him. "I like you. More than I want to. Today, before all that...*crap*...happened. We had a good time together. More than a good time. It was amazing."

She didn't argue. She held his gaze. "What about Kaylee?"

He snorted. "I don't know how many more ways I can tell you that's over. It's been over for a year. I'm going to have to get a restraining order against her—get tough. I should have pressed charges today. I regret that now."

"She's scary."

"She won't hurt you. I've got your back."

She thought that over. "How can I go home with you? You don't have a home."

She had a point. "I'm going to work on that. But for now, I'm at my brother's. He won't care if you stay with me."

She looked unsure.

"Trent's really a teddy bear. Trust me, he'll be fine with it. He's happy as hell that I'm finally letting that house go." He pulled her closer to him, his lips hovering near hers. "Will it hurt if I kiss you?"

She exhaled, slowly shaking her head.

He closed the distance between them, his lips gently covering hers. Their noses bumped as he deepened the kiss. His tongue slid against hers, his fingers tangling in her hair. When he encountered the bump on the back of her head, she stiffened and winced.

"Sorry." He pulled back and loosened his grip. "You should really get that looked at."

"It's a bump. I'll be fine." She put some space between them.

"Why don't you get some stuff together? I'll wait for you out here."

She stared at him, her expression laced with uncertainty.

"I want you to come with me, Aria."

The words seemed to satisfy her. She pulled herself from the couch and disappeared down the hallway.

16

Aria stared up at the ceiling. It was late, or early, depending on how one looked at things. It was nearly three in the morning.

After locking up her house, she had followed Casey over to his brother's house, which it turned out wasn't far from her own. Basically, a mile or two.

His place was nice—a rambler with three bedrooms.

Her first impression of Trent Gage was that he was intense. He was tall—taller than Casey. And far more intimidating. Casey was easygoing and friendly. Trent was mysterious and somewhat elusive in nature. When he and Aria had met, he hadn't smiled, he hadn't frowned. He'd offered her his hand politely — told her his place was her place and that she should make herself at home. But he'd also put off a very protective stance. He had his brother's back, in other words. He was watching her. After what Kaylee had done, she couldn't say she blamed him. She was a stranger to him. He obviously didn't trust her yet.

Turning onto her side, she looked to the spot next to her where Casey was sleeping soundly. He was on his back, an arm flung over his eyes as he slept. He'd stripped down to a pair of boxers before they'd climbed into bed so his chest was bare. She found herself admiring it, even though she knew that wasn't a good idea.

She was getting in over her head with him. All the warnings she'd given herself earlier about keeping him at an arm's length were tossed by the wayside.

When he'd shown up at her house the night before, she'd felt a sense of panic at first. Kaylee was his ex after all. But once she'd worked her way through the initial shock of the situation, his presence had given her some comfort. She knew he'd meant it when he'd told her he wouldn't let Kaylee hurt her. The truth was, at this point, she was worried about Kaylee hurting him.

"Why are you awake?"

His voice startled her and their eyes met. He was awake, too, she realized. He turned over so they faced each other.

"I told you I don't sleep well." She tucked her hands underneath her chin and winced. The bruise on her cheek was a doozy.

"You want some ice for that?"

"No. I'll be okay. Go back to sleep. You have to work in a few hours." She knew he went on shift at seven that morning.

"So do you."

"I don't run into burning buildings for a living. I can be tired and still teach kindergarten."

"I'll be okay. I'm used to sleeping sparsely. Occupational hazard."

They looked at each other for a long time. When he leaned forward, his mouth brushing against hers, she opened for him automatically. His tongue melted against hers as he reached for her, pulling her tighter against him.

Kissing him was an experience. She'd been with other men in her life, but none were like Casey Gage. He knew how to kiss. And she was quickly becoming addicted to those kisses.

She drifted her hands up his chest, over the light coat of hair there, and then higher, until she found his face. He had a thick coat of stubble on his jaw and she suddenly found that very erotic. She nuzzled her nose against it, inhaling his scent.

Somehow he rolled until she was on top of him, straddling his waist. "I don't want to hurt you."

She leaned over, resting her hands on his chest. "I'm a little bruised, Casey. Not broken."

His fingers lifted her night shirt, pulling until he had it up and over her head. Then he palmed her breasts. She inhaled and held the breath, her eyes closing as he kneaded her gently.

She leaned over and crushed her mouth against his a moment later. Their tongues thrashed together and she didn't bother holding back the moan that escaped when he reached for her panties, quickly moving them aside. The minute he touched her intimately, she went up in smoke. Her hips grinded against his and he let out a groan of his own, turning and flipping her onto her back again.

Any clothes between them were quickly discarded. He moved between her legs, stopping at the last minute. "I don't have a condom. I left a lot of my stuff back at the house—"

"I'm on the pill. It's okay."

"I'm clean. I get checked out pretty consistently because of my job."

"I'm clean, too. You're the first guy I've been with in a long time."

He slid forward and gave them what they both wanted. The contact felt heavenly and Aria arched her back, her legs wrapping around him tightly.

He moved in and out, his arms braced on either side of her head. He ran his lips over her neck, up to her ear where he nipped at her earlobe, then used his tongue to soothe the spot.

"I can't get enough of you." He spoke the words softly against her ear and she felt herself begin to unravel. He must have sensed her climax because he started moving harder, faster. She couldn't stop herself from coming undone. He did the same, seconds later, holding himself inside her.

He collapsed against her chest, breathing hard.

She ran her fingers through his hair, content just to hold him — to keep him against her.

He lifted his head. His mouth drifted over hers. Then he levered himself up and rolled over, taking her with him.

"That was..." His voice trailed off.

"Amazing," she finished for him, snuggling against his side.

"More than amazing." He blew out a breath, relaxing his arm so that it rested behind her head.

"You're sweaty." She grinned, running a hand over his chest, where beads of sweat were collecting.

"You're beautiful." His eyes met hers. She could tell he meant the words and her heart clenched. She knew she was in big trouble here. Things with them had skidded out of control very quickly. None of this was in her character. She was cautious with men. She rarely even dated. Yet, here she was, in bed with a man she'd only met a few days ago. And she wanted to stay there.

"We could both call in sick," he suggested, a mischievous grin on his face.

"I wish I could," she said wistfully.

"Aria?"

She lifted her head, looked into his face.

"I know this thing with Kaylee has you scared. But give me a chance to fix it, okay?"

She wasn't sure what he was saying.

"Don't run."

The words were simple and to the point. She rested her chin on his chest as she contemplated him. "I'm afraid she's going to try to hurt you."

He shook his head. "I can handle her. It's you I'm worried about. If I was smart, I'd cut you loose for your own good." He ran his fingers gently down the line of her jaw. "But I don't want to."

"We've only known each other for a few days. How did this happen?" She finally asked.

"I don't know. I guess lightening just strikes that way sometimes."

She found herself smiling at the words. "That was very poetic, Mr. Gage."

"I told you I'm charming that way."

She slid up and over, straddling him again. Before long, they were engrossed in each other and on to round two. By the time they fell asleep, it was after five. Casey's alarm went off an hour later.

She groaned, turning over and reaching for him when he tried to get out of bed.

"I have to go to work, baby."

"So do I. But I don't want to."

He chuckled at that, leaning over and nuzzling her neck. He gave her a thorough kiss, then lifted up and off the bed. "You can use the shower—my shampoo and soap if you need it. Trent's got stuff in there, too. Hopefully you won't mind smelling like a guy today."

She burrowed against the pillows, watching as he dragged a pair of boxers on. "Casey?"

He glanced at her.

"Thank you."

He narrowed his eyes. "For what? All I've done is add to the chaos in your life."

"You were there last night. It helped. I was really scared. I wouldn't have wanted to be with anyone else."

He looked stunned for a moment. Slowly relaxing, he stepped to the bed again and bent, his expression serious as he looked at her. "I wouldn't have, either." He kissed her again, twice, firmly on the lips. Then he winked at her and backed up. "I'm going to go make some coffee."

She watched him leave, wishing she could burrow under the covers and stay there until all the stress in her life disappeared. But she knew she couldn't. She had to go to work—and she had to figure out what to do about her mother—what to do about the kids.

17

When Casey walked into the kitchen, fully dressed, twenty minutes later, he found Trent already there glaring down at the coffee pot. He was ready for shift as well. He eyed Casey only for a second, then shook his head but remained silent.

"What?"

"The walls in this place aren't the thickest," was all he said.

Casey winced. "Shit. Sorry."

Trent leaned back against the counter. "Where is she?"

"In the shower."

"I hope you're being careful here, dude."

"Thanks, Dad," was all Casey said. He dug into the fridge for some orange juice.

"I'm not trying to be Dad. He probably would have lectured the shit out of you *before* you did anything stupid."

"I'm thirty-two years old, Trent. I don't need to explain myself to you."

"I'm not asking you to. But this thing with Kaylee is serious now. For you and for Aria. What do you plan to do about that?"

Casey tensed. "She's not going to hurt Aria."

"She might have already tried."

That was a fact. Casey couldn't argue it. "I'm going to have her file a restraining order. I will, too. Nick will get that stuff going. If she comes near either one of us again, she's going to jail."

Trent remained silent.

"What more can I do?"

"You should have put her in jail for assault yesterday."

"Hindsight's twenty/twenty," was all Casey said.

Trent just grunted.

Aria rounded the corner a minute later. She was dressed for work in a nice pair of pants and a dark colored blouse. Apparently she'd made do with the toiletries in the bathroom because her hair was dry and styled. She'd covered up the bruises on her face for the most part with makeup. She looked at Trent a little uncertainly.

Casey shot him a look.

Trent's shoulders relaxed a little. "Help yourself to whatever...if you're hungry."

Casey supposed that was Trent's way of making an effort. "I'm having cereal. You want some?"

"Just coffee. I need to get going."

"You should be careful today," Trent surprised both of them by saying to her.

She considered him. "I plan to."

He just nodded and turned back to the coffee pot.

She looked at Casey. He gave her an apologetic look. "He's the ass of the family."

Trent turned, shooting a glare Casey's way. Then he looked at Aria again. "You want to clear the air here?"

Startled, she raised a brow at him. "I don't know. You seem very intense."

Casey started to intervene until he saw his brother's lips quirk. Trent was biting back a smile. Point one for Aria.

"I can be. I don't know you. You don't know me. He likes you." Trent tossed Casey a look. "Obviously you like him. I can respect that and mind my manners. And as long as he wants you here, you're welcome here. Just know that I'm paying attention."

Casey muttered an oath.

Aria cracked a smile, surprising him.

"You're a good older brother. I wish I could have been that way for my sister. If I had, she might be alive today." She walked over and stood on her tip toes, giving Casey a quick kiss on the mouth. "I've got to go or I'll be late." She was gone a moment later.

Trent looked a little stunned. Then he smiled halfway and poured himself some coffee.

"Really?" Casey retorted, glaring.

"I like her, little brother. You may have yourself a keeper this time. Don't fuck it up."

. . .

Aria was only at school for an hour when her cell phone rang. She saw Nick Holt's number pop up on the screen and immediately tensed. She knew she needed to take the call, so she stepped into the hallway and answered it.

"Do you have Kaylee in custody?" she asked, in greeting.

He didn't answer right away.

"Hello?"

"No, I don't have Kaylee in custody. But I'm not calling about her. Aria, we have a problem at the hospital. You need to get over here right away."

"I'm at work," she said automatically. "I'm in the middle of class."

"The kids are gone."

Aria felt her heart stop. "What did you say?"

"I'm going to need you to get over here as quickly as you can. Find a sub. Whatever. Just get here." He disconnected, leaving Aria staring at her phone in shock.

It took her a few minutes to find someone to cover her class for the day. Then she headed straight for the hospital, praying the entire way that she'd misunderstood Nick Holt. The kids couldn't be gone. They were still recovering. They weren't physically able to leave the hospital. At least Jaden wasn't.

A sick feeling overcame Aria.

The moment she walked out of the elevator on the third floor, she knew she hadn't misunderstood a thing. There were policemen everywhere. The hallway was crawling with them.

Feeling a swarm of panic, Aria hurried toward the kids' room. She got about halfway down the hallway when she was stopped by a uniformed officer.

"You can't go any further, ma'am. This area is cordoned off for the time-being."

"My niece and nephew are missing," she snapped, trying to shove past him. He held her fast, reaching up and pushing a button on the radio that was attached to his shoulder. "Where's Holt?" he asked into the device. "The aunt's here."

She started to sweat. "What is going on? What happened?"

"I think it would be better if you speak with Detective Holt. He's in charge of this situation."

She began to panic, despite the fact that she was doing everything in her power to prevent that. After what had happened to her the night before…

"Aria."

Nick Holt walked up, indicating the officer let her through. His expression spoke a thousand words.

Aria felt a little faint. "The kids can't be gone."

He took her arm, led her over to a waiting room chair and forced her to sit down. Then he sat down next to her. "Nurse went in a couple of hours ago to do vitals and found both of their beds empty."

Her first reaction was to argue. "That's not possible. They're still recovering. And there's an officer on their door. They wouldn't be able to just walk out of the room without him noticing."

"He was in the bathroom across the hall. He was gone for maybe five minutes. When he got back…"

"I don't believe this! He shouldn't have left them alone for even five minutes! Why didn't he have a nurse in there with them while he was gone?"

Nick looked sheepish. "I don't know. The bottom line is that we've done a thorough search of the hospital. They're not in the building."

Aria took a moment and forced herself to breathe in and out.

"Do you know where your mother is?"

She gathered her wits and thought about that. "I have no idea. She didn't tell me where she's staying—I didn't ask." She met his gaze. "You think maybe she's responsible for this?"

"She wants custody of the kids. Now they're gone. That's suspicious."

It was, now that he mentioned it. She wished she knew her mother well enough to know what she was capable of, but the sad truth was that she didn't. Kidnapping was desperate—unfathomable, considering the fact that Adele had no legal right to the children. But Adele had been desperate and unfathomable in the past.

"I don't think she has a lot of money. I would imagine she probably has a cheap motel room somewhere."

He nodded and lifted his phone, giving an order into it a moment later. Then he gave her his full attention again. "Is there a chance that the kids would have run away on their own?"

"No!" she said automatically.

"Tiffany's been upset. You and I both know that."

Tiffany had been upset. In fact, upset was an understatement. And the fight that Aria and Adele had had the morning before probably hadn't helped things. Adele had insisted on discussing custody of the children in the room where they were sleeping. Past experience told Aria that Tiffany heard things even when she was supposedly out for the count.

"Look, we've got units all over looking for them. We'll find them." He gave her a reassuring look. "In the meantime, I need you to tell me if you think of anything that might help us locate your mother. I need to figure out if she's involved in this in any way."

"What if she's not?" Aria asked, fear sliding through her. "What if someone else took them?"

"We have no proof that's the case. Just try not to panic."

"I can't try not to panic! My sister's kids are missing! After what happened to me last night…" She shook her head. "What if that same person came here and took the kids?"

"That's unlikely. If the kids had been kidnapped by a stranger, chances are they would have made noise. There were plenty of nurses on staff on this floor this morning. They would have heard a commotion like that."

Aria wanted to believe that was true.

"Look, I know it's not easy to remain calm in a situation like this, but I promise you we're doing everything in our power to find the kids—and we will. You can trust me on that."

She forced herself to nod, knowing there was nothing else she could do.

"You asked me about Kaylee earlier. I can update you on that situation if you want."

"You said she's not in custody. Why?"

"I had her hauled in last night. She had an alibi for the time of the attack on you. She was with another doctor that works here in the hospital. I'm pretty sure he's not lying because he claims it took him hours to get rid of her last night. She was hysterical and refusing to leave his house. He damn near called the cops on her himself."

Aria wasn't sure whether this news should relieve her or terrify her more. If Kaylee hadn't been the one to attack her the night before, then who had?

"I spoke to the attorney you mentioned, too. Armbrust. He backed up your story. He said Kaylee wasn't anywhere around when he left your house. His alibi checks out, too. He was home with his wife."

Aria hadn't really considered Brad Armbrust a viable suspect anyway. He had no real motive to hurt her.

"Listen, just because Kaylee wasn't the one who actually attacked you, doesn't mean you should ignore her all together. I'm still getting a bad vibe off of her. She's pretty obsessed with Casey. I already let him know he needs to look into getting a restraining order. You should, too. Just precautionary. It should dissuade her from bothering you anymore." He expression was laced with understanding. "I know with everything you have going on, it's inconvenient for you to deal with, but..."

"I'll check into it," she assured him. She knew he was right. Kaylee may not have attacked her the night before, but the woman was going to be a problem nonetheless.

He stood. "I should go check in with my guys. Just sit tight and I'll be right back."

She watched him disappear into the throng of officers that were still littering the area. She leaned over, her head in her hands, and gave into the urge to say a prayer. At this point, she wasn't sure what else she could do.

"What is going on here?"

Aria lifted her head at the sound of her mother's voice. She jumped to her feet the moment she saw Adele step foot into the waiting room. "Where are they?"

"Where are *who?*" Adele asked, her brow furrowed.

Aria had never been all that good at reading her mother's moods. She was like a time bomb, ticking quietly and then suddenly exploding without warning. "The kids, Mother. Where are the kids?"

"What do you mean, where are they? They're in their room, of course."

"They're not. They disappeared early this morning. They've been missing for hours."

Adele appeared honestly shocked, which scared the hell out of Aria. "That can't be. They were fine when I left them last night. There's an officer on the door—"

"He stepped away to use the bathroom. They disappeared before he got back."

Adele just shook her head.

Aria struggled to decipher whether Adele was lying or not. It was impossible to tell. "The police want to speak to you." The words came out clipped.

Adele suddenly seemed to make sense out of things. "You told them *I* took the kids?" She looked genuinely perplexed.

"I didn't tell them any such thing. They asked me where you were. You haven't exactly been forthright with your situation so I didn't have an answer for them. Naturally, since you threatened me yesterday about wanting the kids, they were suspicious."

"I'm not stupid enough to *steal* the kids,"

Adele said indignantly. She seemed to look closer at Aria suddenly. "What happened to your face?"

"I was attacked last night," Aria answered, still watching her mother closely. "At my house. Someone broke in."

"Oh my God. Are you okay?"

"I'm here," Aria replied.

Nick walked up at that moment. "Mrs. Carlisle. I'd like to speak with you, if you don't mind."

"I did not take the children," Adele said immediately. "I would never kidnap a child. *Any child.* The whole idea of that is preposterous."

"I still have more questions for you. Will you come with me, please?"

Adele looked as though she wanted to protest. Eventually, she sighed, and followed Nick down the hallway.

18

Aria stared at the television screen. Another picture of her niece and nephew flashed by. The Amber Alert alarm sounded. All evening, the warnings had been broadcasted, and still, nobody had seen hide nor hair of either child.

Aria sat in Trent's living room. She'd spoken with Casey earlier and he'd advised her against going to her own house — especially in light of the fact that whoever had attacked her the night before was still on the loose. He was on shift — would be until the following morning. He'd sent his brother, Brandon, to sit with her until he could get home himself. He didn't want her alone — for more reasons than one, he'd said.

She knew he was still on edge about Kaylee. While he'd gone into the police station and filed a restraining order against his ex that morning, Aria hadn't had the time. She'd been tied up at the hospital all day. By the time she'd left there, the courthouse had been closed.

So here she sat, with a baby sitter and one hell of a headache.

"You want something to eat?" Brandon asked, helping himself to a handful of chips from the bag he had stowed in his lap.

Brandon Gage was friendly and likeable. Under normal circumstances, Aria would have enjoyed getting to know Casey's younger brother. But today was not a good day for that. She was agitated and on edge.

She shook her head at him. "No, thanks."

"I'm starved. Maybe I'll make a sandwich."

She shrugged at that.

He got up and disappeared into the kitchen. She continued to sit there and stew.

She thought back to her confrontation with her mother at the hospital. The police hadn't gotten any farther with Adele than Aria had gotten herself. Her mother was claiming complete innocence. She was insulted and upset that anyone was even considering pointing the finger at her. All she'd done was try to help the children—protect them—since she'd gotten here. Those were her words.

Aria had to admit she was doubting her mother's involvement with every moment that went by. For one thing, Adele had planted herself firmly in a chair at the police station. Nick had called Aria twice now, updating her on things. Both times, he'd mentioned Adele hanging around, adamant that she wasn't leaving until the police did their jobs and found the kids. If Adele were responsible for the children's disappearance, it seemed unlikely that she would continue to hang around the police station. Not only that, she'd agreed to, taken, and passed, a polygraph test.

Aria knew those things weren't always a hundred percent, but according to Nick, Adele had been truthful.

So where were the kids? Had they run away on their own? Had someone else taken them? — the man who had murdered their parents?

That thought made Aria's skin chill.

She thought back to every conversation she'd had with Tiffany and Jaden over the past weeks. Their talks had been sparse. The kids had been traumatized — too ill to really speak a whole lot.

Still, Aria thought about the night Tiffany had suffered that terrible nightmare — the one about the bad man who wanted to hurt her. That had been the night Jaden had opened his eyes for the first time since the fire.

Both kids had been terrified that evening — convinced someone had tried to come into their room and hurt them. Tiffany had been pretty much hysterical.

Suddenly Aria frowned. Something Tiffany had said during her breakdown that night stuck out.

I want to go home…

Straightening, Aria grabbed her phone and dialed Nick's number. He didn't answer. She left him a quick message and grabbed the keys to her car.

"What are you doing?" Brandon asked, stepping back into the living room.

"I think I might know where the kids are," was all she said, already heading for the door.

"Did you call Nick?"

"He didn't answer. I left him a message. I have to go."

"That's not a good idea. Casey told me to stay with you."

She sent him an exasperated look. "Then come with me if you want, but hurry up."

He glanced at the sandwich he'd just made longingly. Grumbling under his breath, he set it down on the coffee table and followed her toward the door.

Aria paid little attention to the speed limit as she barreled across town and up into the hills.

"You're going to get pulled over," Brandon warned from beside her, a scowl on his face. "Where the hell did you learn how to drive?"

She ignored him. She didn't give a rip about the speed limit. Somehow she knew time was of the essence.

She glanced at the map app on her phone. According to it, she was two minutes from her destination.

She took a right turn and drove two more miles. About a half mile down the road, to the left, was a sign that read *Briarwood*.

A light seemed to go on inside of Brandon's head. "You think the kids went home?"

"If they ran away on their own—which I'm starting to think they did—this is the only place I can think of that they would go. It's the only place they know."

Brandon appeared to think that over. "You might have something. We should wait for Nick."

"I can't. They're probably scared and alone. I don't want them to get frightened off by a bunch of strangers showing up. Just let me check the place out and see if they're there." She crept the car down each street. She knew her sister's home was going to stick out like a sore thumb. The houses in this neighborhood were all new. They screamed high class wealth. Most of them had at least three-car garages. Some had wrought iron gates separating their driveways from the street.

Aria found herself getting a bit more of a

glimpse into the lifestyle her sister had been leading. It seemed surreal, after the way they had both grown up.

About halfway down the third street, Aria found what she was searching for. The house was ominous. It was obvious that at one time it had been as big and as beautiful as its neighboring homes. But now it was tarnished with black soot. There was yellow crime scene tape wrapped all around its exterior.

Aria felt a chill as she was reminded that this was where her sister had died.

Before Brandon could say a word, she pulled the car to a stop and climbed out of her vehicle.

"Hey, wait a minute. This isn't a safe situation. The house has a lot of structural damage. You can't be walking around in there."

"I don't have a choice," she said, continuing her way up the walk. The front windows had been broken and destroyed, the doorway boarded shut.

Aria took a deep breath, gazing around the yard for any sign that the children were here somewhere. She saw none. Everything was quiet. Eerily quiet.

"I'm going to call Nick again," Brandon said, pulling his cell out of his pocket.

"I'm going to check around back—see if there's any sign that someone could be inside the house." She didn't wait for Brandon to respond. She made her way around the side of the yard, past a group of rose bushes. Just beyond them was a gate that was swinging haphazardly in the wind. She pushed through it and into one of the largest backyards she'd ever seen.

While the house was pretty much destroyed, the backyard appeared untouched. It was perfectly manicured, with a nice patio and expensive looking outdoor furniture, including a built-in, state-of-the-art grill. There was a shed toward the back of the property that Aria figured probably housed yard tools and that sort of thing. A slew of trees spattered the area, protecting it from the late afternoon sunshine.

Aria glanced from one end of the yard to the other. She saw no sign that anyone had been here in quite some time.

Listening to the sounds around her, she felt chilled for some reason. There wasn't so much as a bird chirping or a bee buzzing. It was odd, considering the time of day.

She started to turn back toward the front yard when suddenly a noise cut through the silence. It sounded like...*crying*.

Turning, Aria's eyes scanned the area around her a second time. Nothing stirred.

She heard crying again—more like soft whimpering. She walked toward the back of the property, still unable to pinpoint where the noise was coming from.

She stopped abruptly when she heard the crying a third time. Now it seemed like it was coming from directly above her. She tilted her head up. It took her a moment to figure out what she was seeing. The structure was hidden well within the thicket of trees.

A treehouse.

She glanced at the bottom of the tree she stood near and saw the boarded ladder that was nailed to the tree trunk. She hurried toward it, making quick work of climbing it. When her head poked up through a square that had been cut out of the wooden base of the treehouse, she caught sight of two small, very scared children huddled in the far corner. A strong sense of relief washed over her, and she said a prayer of thanks.

"Please don't send us away," Tiffany begged, holding onto her brother tightly. "We'll go with Grandma. Just please let us stay together."

Aria felt her heart break. She realized at that moment, this was all her fault. "You're not going to be separated. I promise." She climbed the rest of the way into the structure and let out a sigh once she was safely inside. "I'm sorry if you didn't understand things. I'm not sending you away. I want you to come and live with me."

Tiffany looked surprised. Jaden still looked scared.

"You have a lot of people out searching for you," Aria said quietly, walking closer to the children. "You shouldn't have run off that way. How did you get here? It's miles from the hospital."

"We took a cab," Tiffany said quietly, avoiding Aria's gaze. "Like I've seen on television. I stole money from Grandma's purse. I know she's going to be mad, but I had to. It was the only way to get us here."

"We had to run away," Jaden added. "He was going to come back. Nobody believed us."

Aria felt her skin chill again. "You're talking about the bad man again. The one in your nightmare."

"It wasn't a dream.," Tiffany argued, a tear rolling down her cheek. "I tried to tell you, but you wouldn't listen. I tried to tell the nurse, too. He was real. He came into our room that night. He was going to hurt us. I screamed and scared him away. But he promised he was going to come back."

"Who, Tiffany?"

"You should have believed them." The male voice spoke from behind Aria, shocking her into whirling around.

A shiver of terror shot down her spine. A man was hefting himself up and into the treehouse. He had a gun clenched tightly in his fingers.

Aria backed away from him, her first instinct to protect the children. "Who are you?"

"You know who I am, Aria."

She started to shake her head. And then he stepped into a sliver of light that spiked through the window of the tree house. His face came into view. Her heart stopped, nearly dying inside of her chest.

"Michael." The name slipped off her tongue painfully and she almost couldn't believe what she was seeing.

It had been over twenty years since she'd set eyes on her older brother. He'd been eighteen years old when he'd left for the Army. She'd been nine at the time.

And now, here he was, standing in front of her with a gun in his hand.

The last time she'd seen Michael, he'd been a boy. Blonde and blue eyed, he'd stood a few inches under six feet tall. He'd been lanky. While his height looked to be about the same, he'd filled out a bit. His hair had receded to almost nothing. His face was older. He had lines under his eyes and around his mouth. But she knew who he was without a doubt. He had their father's eyes. She'd never forget those eyes.

"You killed Lyla." She spoke the words

softly.

"I had no choice." He walked toward her, reaching out and grabbing her by the arm. He gave her a rough shove so that she landed on her knees near the kids. They both scampered toward her, clearly terrified.

"She was your sister," Aria reminded him.

"A real sister doesn't turn her back on a brother in need."

Aria held the trembling children to her as she struggled to reconcile this man with the boy she'd once known.

"I've been following you for awhile now, sister dear. I'm surprised you didn't notice."

Suddenly things became crystal clear for Aria. "You slashed my tires. You attacked me last night. Why?"

"Because you were getting in the way. I had a loose end to tie up and whenever the opportunity presented itself, there you were. I had to get to the kids—shut them up. You can imagine how things would have been for me if they had started talking. I tried warning them. Just like the little darlings told you, I was in their room one night. But things didn't pan out. The little bitch screamed," he said, glowering at Tiffany, "and I had to take off before I finished the job again. I won't be making that mistake today." He took an ominous step forward.

Aria steeled herself. "They're just children,

Michael. This was never about them. Whatever you're angry about, it was between you and Lyla."

"That's where you're wrong." He shook his head in anger. "When she turned her back on me, it became about her entire family. *She* made that choice."

Aria had no idea what he was talking about. Still, she figured if she could just buy them some time, Brandon would realize she was taking too long to return from the backyard. He would come looking for her. Nick would get the police here. Somehow, help would arrive.

"Your friend's out cold," Michael said, his smile cynical. "I caught him from behind. He never made his call to the cop. But don't worry, he'll live. I have no beef with him."

Aria felt a bit of her hope disintegrate. Obviously Michael had been following her very closely if he'd heard her conversation with Brandon earlier. And now Brandon was hurt.

She tamped her panic down. She'd called Nick before she'd come over here. Hopefully he'd gotten the message and was on his way. Hopefully he had back up with him. Because if he didn't…

"You know, I looked you up, too, Aria. I thought about calling you a few times. I decided against it. You're nothing but a kindergarten teacher. I knew you didn't have a pot to piss in. Lyla, on the other hand, married a rich man. And for a while there, she was happy to see me. She helped me out." He let out a weary sigh. "But when I needed her the most, she turned me away. So I had to *take* the money I needed from her. That's when everything went south."

Suddenly things were starting to make sense to Aria. "She wouldn't give you the money so you broke into her house that night and took it."

"I didn't break in. Her husband let me in. He was all about family—he had none, you know." He shrugged his shoulders. "It doesn't matter now, I suppose. The bottom line is that she refused to get me the money out of the safe so I shot her. Her husband caught on real quick and realized I meant business. But it was too late by then. I knew he'd never keep his mouth shut. So even though he gave me the money—"

"You shot him, too."

"I didn't have a choice. I was planning to leave after that, but I looked up and..." He gazed over at the kids as his voice trailed off. "I didn't want to hurt them. I really didn't. But they'd seen and heard the whole thing."

Aria's stomach felt sick. "So you shot them and set the house on fire."

"I had to think fast. It was the only way to handle things. Sadly, it didn't work. The fire department showed up too quickly and pulled them out. I didn't realize they had survived until a few days later when I saw it on the news."

"They're traumatized, Michael. They won't tell. *I* won't tell. Just let us go." She knew the plea was pointless. She could tell by the evil glare in his eyes that human life meant very little to him.

"Sorry, sis. This is it. The last loose end and I'm out of here. I've already got a ticket to Mexico. Nobody will ever find me."

"They'll find us," she pointed out.

"Doesn't matter. Nobody even knows I had a relationship with Lyla. Not even our dear, old mother. The bitch. I saw her by the way. What a pathetic battleax."

Aria racked her brain for a way to get the kids out of this situation. They couldn't die this way.

"There is no way out. Now I want you to follow me down out of this treehouse and we're going to go for a ride. Keep quiet. No screaming, no sudden movements. I'm going to hold onto a little reassurance." He reached down and yanked Jaden up into his arms.

The little boy immediately started to cry.

"Shut up!" Michael yelled, shaking him violently.

Jaden's crying turned into a mewling noise

as Michael lowered them both out of the treehouse.

"He's going to hurt us," Tiffany whispered, holding onto Aria tightly. Her green eyes were filled with terror.

"Just do as he says unless I tell you differently," Aria said desperately. "I'll figure a way out of this. I promise."

"He has a gun," Tiffany argued.

"You're going to have to trust me, Tiffany. I will find a way out of this." She whispered the words, quickly standing and lowering herself through the opening in the treehouse floor. She could see Michael and Jaden waiting for her on the grass below. Michael had the gun trained on Jaden's forehead.

Aria started to sweat again. God, how was she going to get them out of this?

"Hurry up!" Michael hissed.

Aria used the ladder, then stepped to the grass with a thump. Tiffany reluctantly did the same thing.

"Now go," Michael instructed quietly, giving Aria a shove.

She hesitated. For some reason a strange feeling washed over her. She peered around, the hairs on the back of her neck standing on end, the same way as they had the night before when she'd been attacked. She didn't see anyone around. Just trees, thick and overwhelming, from one end of the yard to the other.

"Move!" Michael snapped, putting Jaden on the ground and giving Aria a rough shove.

When the gunshot rang out, she had no idea where it came from—only that a bullet hit Michael squarely in the middle of his forehead. He fell backward, hitting the grass with a thud.

Police swarmed the backyard within seconds, guns drawn. An officer dropped to his knees and checked Michael's pulse. He shook his head, reaching for his radio. "He's down, Holt. You got him."

"10-4," was the response from the radio.

The children scampered to Aria, wrapping their tiny arms around her tightly. She lowered herself to her knees and held them to her. Somehow it felt right to hold them this way. They didn't seem like strangers to her at all anymore. They felt like family. *Her family*. And suddenly she was very thankful to have something left of her sister to hold onto.

19

Six weeks later...

Aria signed the last of the paperwork that Brad Armbrust handed her.

Over the past few weeks, she'd come to know the attorney. He'd handled all the legal paperwork that had to do with guardianship of the kids. He'd also handled the estate paperwork. There was a lot involved and the process had been complicated.

"That should do it," he said, taking the final document she'd signed and shoving it into his file. He gave her a cautious smile. "You're a very rich woman, Ms. Carlisle."

The words rankled. "The money isn't mine. It belongs to the children. I plan to make sure they are the ones that benefit from it."

He considered her, a little surprised. "That's commendable. I guess I might have been wrong about you."

She frowned at that.

He looked a little sheepish. "I'm going to be honest with you. I saw your brother once. He came here to the office. I wasn't positive who he was. He didn't identify himself to me. But he gave Kevin a hard time. I heard the argument between them. It wasn't vicious—not really. Just typical. We all have relatives that come along when the money starts flowing. I assumed that's what he was."

She realized instantly where he was going with this. "And when you saw me the first time, you *assumed* I was after money, too."

He shrugged. "Most people would be. But Daniel informed me you had no idea about the money until you talked to him about the will. He was pretty sure you were telling the truth."

"I *was* telling the truth. None of this has ever been about money for me. I care about those kids and want what's best for them."

"I can see that." He gave her an honest smile this time. "Good luck to you. I hope you and the kids can get through all this and have a good life. It's not going to be easy."

Aria knew that was an understatement. The kids were still a mess. They were in counseling. She had taken them home with her weeks earlier, after a second stay in the hospital. They were improving daily but still had a long recovery ahead of them.

Adele Carlisle had given up on the custody thing, begrudgingly. She was talking about moving to Seattle. She wanted a relationship with the kids—and with Aria.

Aria knew the children liked their grandmother. She wasn't about to stand in the way of them having a relationship with her. As far as her own relationship with Adele went, that was going to take some time.

"By the way, I found something when I was going through the will," Armbrust said suddenly. "It must have gotten stuck in between some papers. It's a letter for you from your sister."

Aria reached over and took the envelope he offered her. Her name was scrawled on the front of it.

"I've attached my card to your copies of the paperwork. If you should need any further help with things, let me know." Armbrust stood, offering her his hand.

She stood, too, shaking it.

She walked out of his office and down the hall to the elevators. Before she pushed the button, she opened the envelope and pulled a piece of pink stationery out, opening it carefully. A photograph fell out, gliding to the floor at her feet. When she reached over and picked it up, she realized what it was.

A long time ago, when they were young, Aria and Lyla had been close. They'd played together daily, while their mother had been drunk and out of commission and their father had been off carousing with other women. They'd really been all each other had at one point. And in this picture, that was apparent. They were sitting on the floor, bowls of ice cream in front of them, their arms around each other. They were both smiling—clearly unaware of the turmoil that had surrounded them at the time.

The picture made Aria smile.

She began to read the letter.

"Dear Aria, If you're reading this, obviously something has happened to me. I realize I've blindsided you with my request that you take my children—that you raise them for me, now that I can't. I plan to look you up, to catch up with you soon. But I'm writing this letter to explain things to you in case I don't get the chance. When I was forced to pick someone to take the kids in case of— well you know in case of what. Anyway, I didn't think twice. I knew you were the one. I looked up to you when I was little. You were my hero. When you went off to college and left the nightmare we had at home behind, you gave me hope, in a way. I was sad to see you go, but I knew you were going to do

great things. And you have. That's all I want for my kids—for them to do great things. You're the person who can show them how to do that. You should know, Mother and I have remained in touch over the years. While she's still not what I would call parent material, she's different than she was. She's been through treatment. I told her she wasn't going to be allowed to see the kids unless she got help, and she did. I know you have a lot of water under the bridge with her. I did, too. But she's faced her demons. She wants to make amends. Lastly, Michael. The main reason I'm writing this is because I need to warn you about something. If you are reading this, clearly I'm gone. Kevin's gone. And that most likely can be traced back to our brother. About six months ago, he came to me for money. I was happy to see him. I gave him what he asked for. He's come back for more several times. I'm worried. Kevin's convinced he'll go away with time, but I'm not so sure. If anything happens to us—anything at all—I need you to give this letter to the police. Michael's got problems. He saw things during his time at war that changed him. I don't know what else to say. Except thank you. For sacrificing and taking care of Tiffany and Jaden. They're the lights of my life. I love them with all of my heart and I pray that you'll be able to love them the same way. Lyla."

Aria felt a tear dribble down her cheek. She swiped at it quickly, folding the letter up and shoving it back into the envelope. She couldn't help but think how much easier things would have been if this letter hadn't gotten lost. They would have known right away that Michael was the person responsible for the attack on the Cowell family. The police could have hunted him down immediately. Tiffany and Jaden could have been spared some of the turmoil they'd been through.

She supposed there was one good thing to come out of all this. She had met Casey. They were together now. Though they were taking things slowly, they had slid into a comfortable routine. Kaylee had given up on Casey finally. She'd allowed him to buy her out of the home they'd owned together. She'd gotten a transfer and moved to Spokane and Casey was back in his house. Aria was back in hers with the kids. And they were taking things day by day.

"I thought you got lost or something."

She looked up and saw Casey stepping out of the elevator. His expression turned concerned when he saw the tears on her face. "What happened?"

"My sister wrote me a letter." She wiped her eyes again. "Even though I hadn't seen her in a while…" She shrugged her shoulders, sniffling a little as she held the snapshot her sister had given her up for him to see.

He chuckled. "You two were cute kids." He

reached for her, pulling her up against his chest and wrapping her in his arms.

She stayed there for a long time, taking the comfort he offered her. Then she backed up, reaching for the button on the elevator. "Thank you for being here. For the past six weeks. This has been...challenging."

"You've helped me through a few challenges of my own." They both stepped into the elevator when the doors opened. He pushed the button for the lobby.

"So what now?"

He shrugged. "We take things one step at a time. We'll figure it out. The important thing is that we're together."

That was the important thing.

"If I tell you that I love you, is that going to scare you off?"

She was stunned into silence. She met his gaze, almost thinking she'd heard him wrong. She could tell by the sincerity in his eyes that she hadn't. And she realized instantly that she felt the same way about him. "If I tell you the same thing, is it going to scare you?"

He folded his arms over his chest, his brow arched. "I don't know. Give it a try."

She didn't hesitate. "I love you."

He stepped toward her, framing her face with his hands. His mouth covered hers quickly, the kiss deepening without preamble.

The elevator pinged and he slowly pulled away, his eyes never leaving hers. "Does that answer your question?"

Without a doubt, it had.

. . .

Colby Gage sat in her car, trying to stop herself from sweating. She was parked outside a drug store. The bag in her lap was staring back at her like it was a person with eyes. The item inside that bag was truly terrifying.

A pregnancy test.

She'd never taken one before — had never had a reason to.

God, she didn't want to have a reason to now. But she knew she did.

Her period was late. Very late. She was irritable — more than usual anyway — and a little on the nauseous side.

She did her best to talk herself out of panicking. Chances were, this was all coincidental.

She was on the pill, for crying out loud. Women didn't get pregnant when they were on the pill. Not when they took the medicine every day without fail.

The longer the pep talk she gave herself, the better she began to feel.

99.9 percent effective.

That statistic echoed inside of her head. Failure was possible, small as the margin for error was.

"Damn it!" She jammed a hand through her hair, tossing the bag to the seat next to her. There was no way in hell she was pregnant. She and Nick had been broken up for months — hadn't been together in...*weeks*.

She felt her skin heat again. She started the car, feeling a little like she was trapped in a fog bank. The drive to her apartment took ten minutes. Once she was safely inside and finally alone, she went into the bathroom and talked herself into completing the testing procedure. Then she sat on the commode and waited...

LOOK FOR
BOOK 2 of SEATTLE 911
TWIST OF FATE
AVAILABLE NOW!

AVAILABLE TITLES BY JENNIFER HAYDEN

HIDE AND SEEK
(Book 1 Hide and Seek Mystery Series)
UNBROKEN
(Book 2 Hide and Seek Mystery Series)
COLLISION
(Book 3 Hide and Seek Mystery Series)
SWEET REVENGE
SAY MERCY
SOUNDS OF NIGHT
ROOT OF ALL EVIL
AFTER THE RAIN
(Book 1 – The Callahan Series)
IN THE EYE OF THE STORM
(Book 2 – The Callahan Series)
AFTERSHOCK
(Book 3 – The Callahan Series)
LESS THAN PERFECT
(Book 4 - The Callahan Series)
DESERT HEAT
(Book 5 – The Callahan Series)
SHATTERED
(Book 6 – The Callahan Series)

JENNIFER HAYDEN

HOPE FOR CHRISTMAS
(Book 1 in Noel, Montana Series)
HEAD OVER HEELS FOR CHRISTMAS
(Book 2 in Noel, Montana Series)
SKELETONS IN THE MIST
BENEATH BURIED SECRETS
HIDDEN MEMORIES
SHAMELESS
ON THIN ICE
MERMAID COVE
(Mermaid Cove Series Book 1)
RED TIDE
(Mermaid Cove Series Book 2)
BREAKWATER
(Mermaid Cove Series Book 3)
MAYHEM AND MISTLETOE
(Mermaid Cove Series Book 4)
HIDEAWAY HALL
LOCKDOWN
CAUGHT IN THE MIDDLE
(Seattle 911 Series Book 1)
TWIST OF FATE
(Seattle 911 Series Book 2)
WWW.JENNIFERHAYDENBOOKS.COM

CPSIA information can be obtained
at www.ICGtesting.com
Printed in the USA
LVHW080337200719
624757LV00031B/526/P

9 781987 561258